Fancy

A Novel By

VANNA B.

This novel is a work of fiction. All names, characters, places and incidents are products of the author's imagination. Any resemblance to actual events or persons, living or dead, is purely coincidental.

Copyright © 2012 Hope Street Publishing, LLC.

All rights reserved. No part of this book may be reprinted or reproduced or utilized in any form or by any electronic, mechanical, or other means, now known or hereafter invented, including photocopying and recording, or in any information storage or retrieval system without permission in writing from the publisher.

ISBN: 978-0-9853515-0-2

Photography and cover design by RJ Jacques. (www.PhotosXRJ.com)

www.VannaBOnline.com
www.Twitter.com/MsVannaB
www.Facebook.com/VannaBOnline

This book is dedicated to all the "Fancys." Never abandon the person you are for the person you want others to see. You might not like who you become.

"The grass is never greener on the other side of YOU."

-Vanna

Acknowledgements

I'd first like to thank our higher power for gifting me with the talent of writing and the perseverance to achieve my dream.

A million thanks to my amazing husband, Rodney for always supporting me 100% in every way. You've been a HUGE help throughout the entire process and I'm so grateful for you!

My little prince, Dylan, you're the reason why I do everything I do! I'm glad I had your sweet face to look at any time I got frustrated and needed to smile.

To my wonderful parents, Cheryl and Howard for their unwavering love and support. Mom, you always knew I'd be a writer…ever since my first book (Ms. Cluck was it?)

To all my awesome friends and family for your feedback and encouragement: you know who you are. Thanks for being my first readers.

To all my fellow writers that provided me with advice and insight, thanks so much for your help.

And to all of you who don't know me but decided to give my book a chance, thank you for reading my work. There is more to come!

Sincerely,
Vanna

Chapter 1

The clicking of high-priced six-inch stiletto heels on uneven pavement echoes through the air. The beautiful Latina woman donning them walks down a dimly lit side street in downtown Philadelphia, as the frigid wind blows scraps of newspaper across the sidewalk. Her dark rinse tailored jeans and cropped black leather jacket fit her frame perfectly; her silhouette is petite yet curvy in just the right places. It is a chilly October Saturday night and the city is buzzing with activity. The woman pulls her pale pink cashmere scarf tighter around her neck and adjusts the Hermès handbag hanging on her shoulder. As she turns the corner onto a busier street, a strong gust of cold wind blows her black waist-length hair, causing it to whip violently behind her. She merges with the other club-hoppers and a group of young bachelors walking behind her get a whiff of her intoxicating scent. The woman and the other walkers are heading to Velvet, Philadelphia's most exclusive and upscale nightclub. One by one they join the long line of people waiting outside the club. The woman bypasses the line and walks up to the door.

With an enthusiastic smile she greets the bouncer checking IDs. He is a massive red-haired man with a shamrock tattooed on the side of his neck, and a crooked nose that looks as if it might have been broken a few times. Her smile is reciprocated with his own broken-toothed grin, and she plants a magenta kiss on his stubbly, unshaven cheek. He opens the door and she and the cashier girl exchange phony grins and hellos as she continues into the crowded club. Making her way through the blaring trance music and flashing strobe lights, she is met with a barrage of nods, waves, smiles and quick hugs from familiar faces. As she walks past the bar, a group of women look her up and down, enviously watching her confident strut. She arrives at the VIP section, and is letting herself through the velvet ropes when someone stops her, grabbing her arm.

"VIP only, mami. Where's ya band?"

She glares in disgust at the large brown hand grabbing her arm and then at the offender's unfamiliar face. Snatching her arm away, she opens her mouth to give him a piece of her mind, but before she can get a word out, another stocky bouncer steps in between them.

"This is Fancy, Steve," he says to the offender. "Doesn't need a band. She's *always* VIP." He then turns to her with an embarrassed look and shrugs. "Fancy, he's new. He didn't know."

"It's cool," she says insincerely, rolling her eyes.

"Sorry, mami," Steve apologizes. "They told me not to let anybody in without a band. Didn't know you were the exception to the rule." He welcomes her in by extending his arm in the direction of plush blue couches and silver ice filled buckets holding champagne bottles. "But uh, why do they call you Fancy?" It was a question she had been asked many times before.

The name Fancy was given to her back in high school, and she's been using it ever since. Over the years she has gotten so used to being Fancy that she can hardly recall her given name, Maribel Alvarez.

Chapter 2

When Maribel started 9th grade at Olney High School, she felt completely out of place. All throughout middle school she had been the smartest student in her class with the best grades, which earned her the antagonizing titles of "nerd" and "teacher's pet." It came as a shock to her teachers when she decided to attend her neighborhood school, Olney, which most regarded as a bad school, especially since she had been accepted to the top three most academic high schools in the city. She chose not to go to those schools because she saw high school as a fresh start – a way to shake the old image everyone had of her. However there she found herself, once again a misfit, and she wanted nothing more than to fit in.

Ironically, the person who ultimately helped Maribel fit in was someone who went out of their way to be an outcast. With her baggy jeans and oversized hooded sweatshirt, someone could easily mistake Shawna for a boy. The fact that she kept her hair in cornrows, wore a baseball cap and went by the name Shawn was even further misleading.

Maribel first became acquainted with Shawn in the school cafeteria during lunch one day. She had just finished scarfing down a burnt slice of public school pizza. As she chewed her last bite she felt a tap on her shoulder.

"You like that free shit?" a raspy voice asked from under the tilted brim of a Phillies fitted hat.

"Um, yea...no...why do you care?"

"I don't. But you should. That shit's from the government. That means it's got all types of toxic shit up in it, and guess who's the fuckin' lab rat. I'da expected someone like you to know that."

"Someone like me? What's that supposed to mean?"

"I'll catch you later, alligator," she said as she coolly strode off.

"Wait, what's your name?" Maribel yelled after her.

"Shawn."

Shawn's comment dwelled in Maribel's thoughts and after school she waited out front, hoping she would see her leaving. While waiting, she sat on a bench watching the interactions between the other students. Everyone seemed to be busy laughing, gossiping, sharing jokes and making plans. Maribel felt like a cold, vapid statue surrounded by vivacity and life. It was as if she didn't even exist.

Her people-watching was interrupted by the sound of quarreling. She recognized Shawn's raspy voice and turned to see her arguing with a school security guard.

"Fuck you, fat ass!" Shawn yelled at the security guard, waving both middle fingers at him.

Maribel sheepishly approached her.

Vanna B.

"Hey, um, what did you mean in the lunch room earlier?" she asked.

"What do you mean 'what did I mean'?" Shawn asked with a chuckle, admiring her own words.

"Well, you said 'someone like me'...something about 'someone like me'."

"Oh, you know, a nerd...a geek...a bookworm...a goody two-shoes."

There were those monikers again. Names habitually used to taunt her, dispirit her and single her out.

"Well look at *you*!" Maribel snapped back. "Who are *you* supposed to be?"

"I ain't *supposed* to be nobody. I'm Shawn. I do my own thing and I gets money." She pulled a large wad of folded bills out of her pocket and Maribel could see that there were at least a few hundred-dollar notes in it.

"What are you, a drug dealer or something?"

"Do I look like a dummy?" Shawn asked, as she smirked and shook her head.

"Then how'd you get all that money?"

"I can show you better than I can tell you." Shawn gestured for Maribel to come with her as she began walking down the street. At first she was hesitant to follow. Although Shawn had certainly piqued her interest, she felt a little apprehensive. She decided that the new Maribel had to brush her fears aside and be adventurous for once. The old Maribel would have immediately dismissed the offer. But that was the geek...the nerd. The new Maribel was not going to play it safe. For once she was going to do what she wanted to do. She was going to appease her curiosity and follow Shawn to wherever she was headed.

With each step they took, the sound of the after-school bustle grew more and more quiet. It was a rather windy September afternoon, but the sun was shining brightly, lending its glowing warmth.

"So you gonna tell me your name?" Shawn asked, finally breaking the silence.

"Maribel."

After a short walk they arrived at a two-story brick row home, on a narrow one-way street. There were bars on the windows and the cement on the steps was cracked and crumbling. The porch floor was covered with soiled AstroTurf and upon it sat a pair of dingy white resin chairs.

"Welcome to mi casa," Shawn said, unlocking the door with a silver key hanging from the blue and gold Olney High School lanyard around her neck. They walked through the door into the living room and were greeted by a fog of cigarette smoke accompanied by the voices of soap opera actors blaring from a small television sitting atop a larger broken floor model. Shawn's mother, a fortyish heavy-set woman, sat on a maroon loveseat sucking on what was left of her Newport. She didn't bother looking up from the TV when they entered, and Shawn didn't bother looking her way either.

Shawn and Maribel proceeded to the staircase but were interrupted by Shawn's mother's throaty voice calling from the sofa.

"Shawna," she said, "I know you ain't bringin' nobody up in my house without introducin' 'em."

After a long huff accompanied by dramatic eye rolling, Shawn reluctantly turned around.

"Mom, Maribel. Maribel, Mom."

"Hi, Maribel. Good to meet you, sweetie. You can call me Ms. Mercer."

"Nice to meet you, Ms. Mercer."

After the brief introductions, Shawn led Maribel up the stairs and into her bedroom, located at the end of the hall in the very back of the house. Shawn's bedroom was small and messy. Her twin bed was unmade and clothes were strewn about. On her dresser sat about twelve different bottles of men's colognes, and the mirror above it was bordered with cut-out celebrity photos, mostly of basketball players and rappers. The wastebasket was overflowing with various snack food wrappers and there seemed to be sneakers everywhere.

"So you brought me here to show me your junky room?" Maribel asked, raising her eyebrows.

"Yeah, what'cha think?" Shawn asked sarcastically in return. "No, actually I wanted to show you this." She threw a black drawstring trash bag onto her unmade bed. "Open it."

Maribel sat down next to the bag and opened it. Rummaging through the bag's contents, she discovered it was all clothing. She began pulling pieces of it out: a cream linen DKNY blouse; a turquoise Juicy Couture track suit; a navy blue and yellow striped men's Polo shirt. Maribel noticed all of the clothing had some sort of designer label.

"What'd you steal all this stuff?" she asked.

Shawn smiled a wide, devilish grin. Although she never owned any designer clothing, Maribel recognized some of the brand names from seeing them worn by the popular kids at school, and others from seeing them in her mother's fashion magazines. She enjoyed reading such magazines and admired the chic clothes and accessories. She once asked her mother for a pair of *Chloé* sunglasses she saw in Harper's Bazaar. Her mother's reply: "You know how much those cost? You better go down to 5th Street and get you some knockoffs."

As Maribel pulled the next item out of the bag her face lit up. "The model in the Guess ad was wearing these!" she exclaimed, holding up a pair of blue snakeskin print pants.

"You like 'em? They're yours," said Shawn.

"Nah, it's okay. They're probably not even my size," Maribel said, looking at the tag on the pants.

"I'll tell you what. You can take them *and* the matching jacket, 'cause you look like you could use some new shit in your wardrobe."

Maribel looked down at her faded blue relaxed fit jeans, then at Shawn, then at her mauve floral button-up sweater, and by the time she looked back up again, Shawn was laughing hysterically. Embarrassed, Maribel crossed her arms and got up to leave.

"Come onnn. My bad, man. You ain't gotta leave."

"Well if all you're gonna do is make fun of me—"

"Nah, I'm sorry. I wasn't tryna hurt your feelings. It's just that you're so pretty and, well...you should be rockin' some fly shit. That sweater right there looks like something somebody's grandma would wear."

Maribel peered at her reflection in the dusty mirror and smiled as she held back a laugh.

"I actually thought the same thing while I was putting it on this morning," she admitted.

The two shared a hearty laugh.

"So you just steal all these clothes and sell 'em?" Maribel asked.

"Yeah, pretty much," Shawn replied, "but that ain't all." She swung her closet door open to reveal bags and boxes full of merchandise. Her closet was overflowing with not only designer clothing, but also handbags, shoes, belts, sunglasses and even jewelry.

"You never got caught?"

"Nope. I'm extra careful. You might even say I'm the best that ever did it."

"Is that the right time?" Maribel asked, pointing to the digital clock radio on the dresser.

"It's a couple minutes slow."

"I better get going."

They walked back down to the living room where Shawn's mother was glued to the same spot on the couch, smoking another Newport, and made their way through the curtain of smoke to the front door.

"Well, thanks for the outfit."

"It's nothing. See you tomorrow."

"See ya."

When Maribel got home she tried on the outfit. It fit her more snugly then she was accustomed to.

"Yeaaah," she said to herself as she turned around to see how her butt looked in the pants. "This is how the *new* Maribel should dress." She was excited about her new outfit and couldn't wait to wear it to school the next day.

The following morning Maribel woke up at 7:06, 24 minutes before her alarm was set to sound. It was a chilly morning, but a hot shower helped warm her up. After brushing her teeth and putting on her underwear and bra, she slipped into her new pants. She loved how the hues of blue faded from a navy to a royal and finally to a baby blue, and she thought the snakeskin pattern looked fierce and edgy. Next she put on a plain black baby tee and the matching snakeskin print jacket. She knew she wouldn't have any suitable shoes, so she went into her mother's room to find something more stylish. *Thank God we're both sevens*, she thought to herself, opening the closet door. She scanned the closet floor for black footwear. *Too dressy*, she thought, inspecting a pair of strappy stilettos. Next, she picked up a faux fur knee boot. *Too silly*, she thought, giggling to herself. Finally she saw a pair of leather ankle boots. "Perfect!" she exclaimed as she began slipping them on. Maribel decided that instead of her usual ponytail, she would leave her hair down to accompany her new look. She grabbed her black canvas book bag from her bedroom floor and headed downstairs to the kitchen where her mother was making coffee.

Maribel's mother, Anna, was a pretty 35-year-old Puerto Rican woman. Her eyes lit up when she saw Maribel.

"Wow, look at you, Mari! Que bonita!" she exclaimed.

Maribel was surprised by her mother's reaction.

"You like my new outfit, Mom?"

"Sí, absolutamente! Where'd you get it?"

"My friend gave it to me. It's Guess."

"Ohhh, I see. You finally got yourself a little boyfriend. Good for you!"

Maribel didn't bother telling her mother that her friend was actually a girl. She was enjoying the attention she was receiving from her. In fact, she couldn't remember the last time her mother was so pleased with her.

Anna was different from most moms. She wasn't big on praise or affection, and stayed preoccupied with her social life for much of Maribel's upbringing. She eventually matured, but during her daughter's teenage years, Anna lived her life as if she, herself, were still a teen. She enjoyed the nightlife, often staying out all night until the early morning hours. Maribel's father left Anna while she was pregnant. It was rumored that he had moved back to his hometown, San Juan, although no one knows for sure. When Maribel was three, Anna had married a doctor twice her age, but they divorced when she discovered he had been carrying on another relationship and had a child on the way. She had been in many relationships since, each more short-lived then the next. Anna was on a never-ending quest for love – and security. She knew that one day she would find her prince charming – who would also happen to be rich – and that he would sweep her off her feet, marry her and fulfill her every want and need. In search of her meal ticket, Anna went on many a date, and was always seen with different men. Her career, or lack thereof, was similar to her love life. She never maintained steady employment for long. Most of her jobs were attained through a local temp agency, including her current position as a receptionist for a small insurance firm. Since she was never into school much herself, she never praised Maribel for her good grades and scholarly achievements. College was never an option for Anna, and because it was so costly, she never considered it for Maribel either. She believed it was more sensible for an attractive woman to simply snag a wealthy man and rely on him to take care of her — only she had not yet successfully been able to do so.

Maribel was glad to finally get some of the much-needed attention she had always wanted from her mother. At the same time, though, it was disheartening to her that the cause of her mother's excitement was something so superficial.

"Mari, viene aquí," Anna said, pulling items from her large leopard print handbag. "You need to learn how to put on make-up."

She began outlining Maribel's almond-shaped eyes with a black eyeliner pencil. Maribel loved having her mother so close to her and was happy to feel her touch, something she hadn't felt in quite some time. Next, Anna put black mascara on Maribel's eyelashes and applied a peach-colored blush to her cheeks with a big, soft brush.

"You look like a Puerto Rican Barbie," she said, stoking the brush along Maribel's cheekbones. "That boyfriend of yours is gonna go crazy when he sees you."

Finally Anna used a shimmery, rosy pink lipstick on Maribel's lips.

"Go like this," she said, rubbing her lips together for her daughter to imitate. "All done." She held up a compact mirror for Maribel to look into before putting her make-up back into her purse.

Maribel wished she could hold on to that moment just a little longer. She didn't know when she would have her mother so close again, or when Anna would be as proud of her as she was now.

"Does, my hair look okay, Mom?" she asked, hoping her mother would offer to style it for her.

But Anna only replied, "It looks fine."

On her way out, Maribel stopped in the dining room and looked in the large wood-framed mirror hanging on the wall. She admired her appearance and smiled at the new Maribel, who was smiling back.

With boys cat-calling and shouting at her from across the street, Maribel's walk to school was quite interesting, but her day turned even more eventful once she arrived at school. All eyes were on her. As she walked through the halls, people turned their heads to watch her pass. Her classmates, who were all surprised to see her new look, crowded around her desk to gawk at her. Even her homeroom teacher told her how beautiful she looked.

When it was lunch time, she bypassed the free lunch line. She didn't think free lunch was something that should be associated with the new Maribel. *From now on*, she thought, *I'm going to buy my lunch*. She stood in the back of the much longer à la carte line and thought about what she would order. When she got up to the register, she ordered chicken fingers, french fries and a can of Sprite. She sat down at her usual table and began eating her food. A couple bites into her chicken fingers someone approached her.

"Hey," said the slim short-haired girl with a mouth full of braces. "I like your make-up." Maribel thanked her and the girl walked away.

Several minutes later a boy walked up to her table. He was very tall and was wearing an Olney High Varsity Basketball jersey. Bending down, he leaned in towards Maribel and said, "My friend wants to know if he can have your number."

This caught Maribel off guard.

She just said the first thing that came to mind: "What kind of guy sends his friend instead of coming over himself?" The tall boy shrugged and walked off.

Next came a well-dressed trio of two girls and a boy. Their heels clicked on the cafeteria floor as they sashayed over, and they were all wearing the same pink glitter lip gloss. One of the girls, who was wearing black sunglasses on top of her head, sat down across from her while the other two students stood at the edge of the table.

"Hi!" said the girl with a big smile, "Are you new?"

"Actually—"

"Yup, she's new," interrupted a familiar raspy voice from her right. Maribel turned to see Shawn taking the seat next to her. Smiling that wide devilish grin of hers, she added, "Her name's *Fancy*."

"Nice to meet you, Fancy. I'm Rasheeda," the girl said, dramatically placing her hand on her chest. "This Asian sensation is my best friend Linda, and this sexy bitch right here is Stefan."

"*Queen* Stefan," he said, holding his hand out as if he expected someone to kiss it. They all shared a good laugh.

Maribel was finally fitting in. She was enjoying her newfound identity and all the attention it was attracting. Gone were the days of her feeling like an outsider looking in. She had successfully shaken her former image and was no longer a nerd or a misfit. For the first time in her life she felt that she was *somebody*. She was *Fancy*.

And she's been Fancy ever since. That is the name everyone knows her by, and the only name she answers to – even her mother calls her Fancy now. She never talks about the old her. Maribel died and was reborn Fancy.

Chapter 3

"Why do they call you Fancy?" the bouncer asks, ushering her into Velvet's VIP section.

"Because I'm fuckin' fancy," she replies, rolling her neck. She flips her hair and walks through the velvet ropes with a switch before slinking through the crowd to her usual table, where her two friends are waiting for her with a bottle of Dom Pérignon on ice.

"Heyyyy!" Fancy says, exchanging hugs with them.

"Hey girl," replies Jaslyn, a tall, thin dark-skinned woman with short, spiky hair. She has the physique of a fashion model and walks accordingly. Wearing head to toe Marc Jacobs, she looks like she just stepped off a Fashion Week runway. Jaslyn is the daughter of an orthopedic surgeon and a state representative. She was raised in a wealthy Delaware suburb and was a spoiled brat growing up. Not much has changed in that aspect. When Jaslyn does not get her way, things can turn very ugly, very fast.

Fancy's other friend, Brittany, is a short, busty bleach blonde with big green eyes. There are frequent debates over whether or not her breasts are real, although she always insists that they are. Tonight, like most other nights, she has them on display in a black and white pin-striped halter vest.

Several straining buttons hold the vest closed, while the topmost one remains unbuttoned. She's paired the vest with black skinny jeans and black leather knee boots with silver chains dangling across them. Brittany was raised in Philly's Kensington section. She and her drug addict mother never got along, so to avoid being around her, Brittany hung in the streets a lot as an adolescent. She was usually the only white girl in a group of all black and Hispanic kids. She is loud and brassy and bites her tongue for no one.

Fancy, Jaslyn and Brittany can always be seen partying together, most often at Velvet, where they all became acquainted last summer. The trio has become a staple at the club, as common as the bouncers and the silver champagne buckets. At a glance, one would think they're the best of friends. But Fancy knows Jaslyn and Brittany won't be around for the long run. They are superficial friends and she is to them exactly what they are to her; simply someone to be seen with. Each of the three women is a stunning beauty, and together their presence is even more intimidating. They never cease turning heads, celebrating lavishly and being the life of the party. Tonight will be no different.

"Let's get this party started!" Jaslyn exclaims, as she pops the cork from the champagne bottle, allowing the foam to spill out. She pours some for each of them and they click their glasses together in a toast. "To us!"

Velvet is completely packed and stops letting people in after exceeding the maximum occupancy. The club's go-go dancers, The Velvet Girls, dance atop pedestals in silver bikini tops and hot pants. Bartenders hustle back and forth behind the bar, attempting to keep up with all the orders. The people in the crowd jump up and down, fist-pumping to the thumping bass, some spilling their drinks. The DJ changes the song to a more up-tempo trance record.

"Ooooh, Tiesto! This is my shit!" Brittany exclaims, jumping out of her seat. She grabs Fancy and Jaslyn by their hands, pulling them up to dance. The remainder of their night consists of wild dancing, plenty of mingling, posing for lots of photos and heavy drinking. After the champagne, Fancy has a shot of tequila, followed by two cosmopolitans, a martini, a shot of vodka and several beers before finally she is so inebriated she has lost track of how much alcohol she's consumed.

Chapter 4

It is the following morning when Fancy is awakened by sunlight streaming through the large windows of a high-rise luxury apartment in Center City Philadelphia. She is completely naked and her head is throbbing. She sits up in bed, realizing she does not know where she is. She looks next to her and sees a bare fair-skinned back and dark brown hair. *Oh God, not again*, she thinks to herself, realizing that she drank too much the previous night and blacked out. This is not the first time it has happened. Fancy has awakened many a morning, unable to recall the events that took place the night before. She hates not being able to remember things she has done and having to rely on others to deliver the embarrassing details. She has heard stories of her singing karaoke, fighting and even flashing people, and has not been able to recall a single minute of those occurrences. This is the first time, however, she has awakened in a stranger's bed, and she feels worse than ever.

As she sits there next to the stranger in his bed, Fancy is overcome with a torrent of emotions. She is worried, angry and afraid all at once. She is worried because it is apparent to her that she has slept with a complete stranger and she can't remember any details about their encounter. She is angry at herself for drinking so heavily after promising herself she would never become so intoxicated again. And she is afraid that if this continues to happen she may very well end up dead.

Tears begin to stream down Fancy's face. She tries to keep quiet so she does not wake the sleeping stranger, but her sobs become louder as she thinks to herself, *I am pathetic*. The stranger begins to stir and is soon awake.

"Hey, what's wrong?" he asks with concern, attempting to put his arm around her to comfort her. She jumps out of bed pulling the sheet to cover herself.

"Who are you?" she asks. "I don't even know your name."

"Sure you do, Fancy," he says in his thick Italian New Yorker accent. "It's me – Tony."

"I was drunk and blacked out. The last thing I remember is dancing with my friends."

"So you don't remember meeting me, or anything that happened after that?

"No, I don't."

"I didn't realize you were that drunk. I mean we were both drinking but you seemed to know what you were doing. I didn't force you to do anything."

"No," she says, sitting back down on the bed, "I'm not implying that. I'm just kinda embarrassed...and mad at myself for getting so drunk."

"I understand. We'll look, why don't you get dressed and I'll take you home."

"Okay."

"And if it's any consolation to you, we had a great night. There's nothing to be embarrassed about."

His words are no consolation at all and Fancy knows that in addition to the walk of shame, she is in for the most awkward car ride ever.

Chapter 5

Fancy and Tony throw their clothes on and take the elevator down to the building's parking garage. When they are both inside of his white Mercedes-Benz, Tony asks Fancy where she lives.

"I'm at the Piazza. You know, the luxury apartments on 2nd and Germantown."

"How do you like it? I heard it's kind of loud and busy over there."

"Sometimes, but it's not bad for $1,800."

"Hey, as long as you like it."

The car pulls out of the garage and the ride is as awkward as Fancy imagined it would be. Tony's several attempts to make conversation are met with blunt responses followed by silence. While Fancy thinks Tony seems like a nice guy, she just isn't in the mood to talk right now.

When Tony's car disappears up the street, Fancy begins to walk briskly, but not into the luxury apartments. Instead, she walks two blocks to 3rd and Girard and waits on the corner at the bus stop. She takes a pair of dark Chanel sunglasses out of her purse and puts them on, hiding her tired eyes. Several minutes later, the bus pulls up and she climbs on board, taking a seat in the very back.

As the bus makes its way north, Fancy gazes out the window, watching the scenery change from trendy cafés and art galleries to run-down bodegas and Chinese stores. The landscape becomes all too familiar as the bus enters the Olney section of the city. It is the same neighborhood Fancy grew up in, and much about it has changed since she was a girl. It was once a predominantly middle class neighborhood with small pockets of lower class areas scattered about. Over the years, those pockets grew and the quality of the neighborhood gradually deteriorated. Olney now consists primarily of impoverished families, and its littered streets are ridden with drugs and crime.

The bus is approaching Fancy's stop at C Street and Rising Sun Avenue. She pulls the cord, signaling the driver to stop. She exits through the back door and begins walking up C Street. As she passes a Chinese store, an elderly man in a tattered coat and fingerless gloves begs her for a dollar in Spanish. She understands him, but ignores his desperate plea and continues walking, her gaze never diverting from the path in front of her.

Finally Fancy arrives at her destination, a dilapidated two-story brick row home that has been converted into two apartments, one of which she resides in. As she ascends the littered cement steps she spots a folded piece of paper stuck in the screen door. She picks it up to discover it is a notice from the gas company stating they had come out earlier that morning and turned off her gas due to nonpayment. Fancy groans as she unlocks the door and walks inside. She picks up the mail scattered on the floor in front of the door and throws it on top of a large pile of unopened mail on the table. Exhausted, and still suffering with a pounding headache, she flops on her frameless bed, which is nothing more than an old mattress atop a beat-up box spring. Her apartment is so cold she doesn't bother taking off her coat. She just curls up and pulls the covers over her head in an attempt to get warm.

Suddenly she is overcome by a wave of nausea and runs to the bathroom to vomit. Afterwards she leans into the sink and splashes her face with icy water. *This shit is getting old*, she thinks to herself, staring in the mirror at her dull, dry skin and the dark circles lurking under her tired eyes. *It's supposed to be fun, so how come I'm not having fun?* Now, at the age of 27, she is finally beginning to grow weary of the party life.

Fancy returns to her bed and lies on her side across it, resting her head on her arm. She peers straight ahead into her door-less closet, which is overflowing with expensive clothes, handbags and shoes: things that help her paint a picture of the person she wants the world to see. But it isn't her. It's all a lie – an elaborate façade that she goes out of her way to maintain. Lately she is finding it more and more difficult to keep up an appearance of glitz and glamour when her reality is one of poverty and struggle. She feels like a Hollywood actress playing an on-screen role, only when the cameras stop rolling, instead of being rich and famous, she is broke and alone. It all started off so easy – so simple and fun.

After making the dramatic transformation to Fancy in high school, she traded books for boys in her attempts to keep up her new image. It was a piece of cake; all she had to do was walk down the street wearing a pair of tight jeans and she could snag a high roller. The local drug dealers had no problem tossing a girl a couple hundred dollars or taking her shopping. This, in fact, was how they went about courting girls. They all remained in competition with one another, and whoever had the prettiest girl in his passenger seat was "the man." By far the most attractive girl in her neighborhood, Fancy instantly became a hot commodity among them. They each desired her and provided her with gifts and money, sometimes taking her on weekend vacations and shopping sprees in their attempts to woo her. Fancy loved keeping her closet full of designer clothes and shoes. It was fun being so young and being able to go on all-expense-paid trips. She enjoyed the luxuries of having her cell phone bill paid and being one of the only girls at school with Gucci and Prada bags.

When she graduated from Olney High, Fancy didn't look into colleges or go job hunting. She figured she would never have to work. Her mother had always told her how much easier it was to simply "use what you got to get what you want," and when Fancy discovered this was true she took full advantage.

Yes, it was simple back then. But lately Fancy has been finding it harder and harder to obtain and keep a man solely for the purpose of providing for her. Her disinterest and true intentions eventually show, and the men soon take off.

Now, nearing 30 years of age, unemployed, in debt and unable to keep up with her bills, Fancy finds herself stuck between a rock and a hard place. Right now she knows the first order of business should be to pay her gas bill, but she doesn't have enough money. She also knows that her rent is due soon and that if she does not pay, her landlord – who is tired of her late payments – will evict her. Fancy needs money – now – and there is only one way she knows how to get it. *I need a man*, she says to herself, *and tonight I'm gonna get one*.

Tonight is the celebrity birthday bash of 76ers point guard Aaron Jameson, and Fancy decides that there is no way she can miss it. But right now all she wants to do is go someplace where she can take a hot shower. She picks up her phone and dials Brittany, who answers on the second ring.

"Hey girl."

"Hey Britt."

"Did you have fun last night? You were all over that hot Italian dude."

"Oh my God, why did you and Jaslyn let me leave with him? I was soooo drunk."

"Duh, we were too, bitch. You seemed like you were feelin' him. We were doing our own thing anyhow."

"Okay. Well, um, I wanted to know if I could crash at your place for a few days. They're doing some renovations in my building and they say I can't be here while it's going on."

"And they're just now telling you? That some bullshit. But yeah, of course you can stay here. You know Aaron Jameson's birthday party is tonight at Velvet, so bring something sexy."

"You know I will. I'm wearing my gold Herve Leger bandage dress."

"Ooooh, yeah, you look bangin' in that dress! Pullin' out the big guns on 'em, huh?"

"Yup, I'm trying to get the birthday boy! On my way now."

"See ya soon."

Chapter 6

Two bus rides and a 10-minute walk later Fancy arrives at Brittany's newly constructed 5-bedroom townhouse in Philadelphia's Far Northeast section.

"Lucky bitch and her damn CEO sugar daddy," she mutters enviously, dragging her two Louis Vuitton luggage bags up the red brick steps. Seeing Brittany's beautiful house makes her wish she had invested in a home instead of buying so many frivolous things.

Fancy has never bothered to think long term. She's never considered saving any money or owning a home. She only thinks about the present – the newest shoe, or what outfit she will wear to the club that night. Instead of thinking about her future, she focuses all her energy into putting on a show for everyone else. Since she came from nothing, appearing successful is enough for her. As long as everyone thinks she is doing great, she is satisfied. Owning expensive things provides a feeling of self-worth for her. But she has become so caught up in *things* that she's lost the only thing that ever really mattered – she has lost herself.

Fancy walks up to Brittany's door and rings the bell. She plasters a fake smile on her face as she waits for the door to open. Several seconds later

Brittany opens the door wearing a pink silk robe and they exchange hugs.

"Hey Fancy. Come on in."

"Thanks for letting me stay on such short notice."

"Anytime. I just think it's kind of weird that your building didn't give you any type of notice beforehand."

"I know, right?"

"You want some coffee? I just made a fresh pot."

"No, thanks. My stomach is still jacked up from all that liquor. I actually just want to shower and sleep a little more, if that's cool."

"Knock yourself out. Shit, after the crazy ass night we had, I could use some more shut-eye myself."

Brittany shows Fancy to one of the guest rooms and tells her to make herself at home. The room is decorated in an old Hollywood theme. All of the décor, from the bedding to the curtains, is black and white with splashes of red here and there. On the walls are black and white photos of movie stars like Marilyn Monroe and Audrey Hepburn. Accents such as the old phonograph, brass alarm clock and antique telephone help complete the look.

Fancy walks into the bedroom's adjoining bathroom, where the old Hollywood theme is continued. There is a brass vanity with large globe lights around the mirror – the kind found in movie star's dressing rooms. Plush black and white towels and red washcloths hang on brass towel bars. There is a deep, old-fashioned claw foot bath tub with a shower and several vintage movie posters.

Fancy decides that in lieu of a shower she will take a warm, soothing bath. She turns the shiny brass handles to begin filling the tub. After undressing, she steps into the bath tub and sits down in the warm water. She leans back and relaxes, letting out a long sigh of relief. It feels good to finally decompress, and she wishes that the bath could wash away her worries, if only for a little while.

Yet even as she relaxes her body, her mind remains anxious. She wonders if Brittany would be as hospitable if she knew who she really was. Would she and Jaslyn still want to be seen with her if they discovered the socialite they've been partying with is, in actuality, a pauper living in the ghetto? Fancy shakes her head in doubt.

As she lathers her body, her mind wanders further and she begins to daydream about the night ahead of her. She envisions herself as Cinderella and the party as the ball. Aaron Jameson is Prince Charming and the two of them dance the night away. They fall deeply in love and he sweeps her off her feet, rescuing her from her glum reality and providing her with everything her heart desires. Then they are married and live happily ever after in a huge castle. Fancy laughs quietly to herself.

She soon realizes the skin on her fingers and toes is wrinkled, and that the bath water is getting cold, indications that she's been soaking in the tub long enough. She steps onto the plush cotton bath rug and wraps a big, fluffy white towel around her body. After drying off and dressing in black boy shorts and an oversized Miami t-shirt, she finally slips into bed for some much-needed sleep.

Chapter 7

Fancy's deep slumber is interrupted by a knock on the door.

"Hey girl, you awake?" Brittany asks, opening the door and turning on the light.

"I am now," Fancy replies drowsily as she sits up in bed rubbing her eyes.

"I brought you a little something," Brittany sings, handing her one of two wine glasses containing a deep red liquid.

"Pre-gaming already, Britt?"

"Already? It's 9:45, Miss Thang. We need to start getting ready so we can leave by 11."

Fancy looks at the clock on the nightstand.

"Damn, I slept all day!"

"Yep. I've only been up for a couple hours myself. We needed to recuperate so we can do it big tonight!"

They laugh and click their glasses together.

"What kind of wine is this anyway?" Fancy asks, preparing to take a sip.

"Cabernet Sauvignon," Brittany replies, exiting the room. "See ya in about an hour."

Fancy reluctantly pushes the warm covers back and steps out of bed, stretching and releasing a big yawn. She opens her duffle bag and pulls out her curling iron and make-up. She begins her make-up regimen by applying concealer. Lately, she has been finding it necessary to use more of it under her eyes. It is getting increasingly difficult to mask the fine lines and dark circles brought on by countless nights of drinking and partying. Next, Fancy uses a honey-colored foundation to even out her blotchy skin tone, and then applies a shimmery bronzer on the apples of her cheeks to add to a bit of a glow to her dulling complexion. After meticulously applying her black eyeliner and mascara, sparkly gold eye shadow and bright red lipstick, she examines her face in the mirror. *Much better*, she thinks to herself. She uses her curling iron to style her long, thick black hair. Moving closer to the mirror, she squints her eyes, attempting to locate a strand of gray hair she had seen only a moment ago. Having found the culprit, she quickly yanks it out before resuming her primping. When she's finished curling her mane, she gives it a quick combing with her fingers and sprays it with what seems like an entire can of holding spray. She coughs uncontrollably, waving her way through the cloud of chemicals as she walks out of the bathroom. Finally, Fancy slips into her form-fitting metallic gold dress and puts on her jewelry: a pair of cascading gold chandelier earrings and a gold costume ring with a huge faux princess cut ruby in it. She carries her nude platform pumps and matching clutch across the hall with her to Brittany's room.

"Hey Britt, can you zip me up?" she asks, turning her back to her.

"Sure," Brittany replies, zipping Fancy's dress. "I fucking *love* this dress."

"Thanks. Yours is hot too! It is new?"

"Yep – Gabanna."

"Niiiice."

Brittany pushes her breasts up and pulls down on the low-cut silver and black leopard spotted dress. She puts on her strappy silver heels, grabs her black quilted leather purse and she and Fancy make their way to the garage where Brittany's shiny ruby red Porsche coupe is parked.

As the Porsche pulls up in front of Velvet, valet attendants dash to open its gleaming doors and the people waiting in line watch to see who will step out. Fancy and Brittany exit the vehicle looking like two movie stars arriving at a film premier. As they walk past the line into the club, the women turn many a head and instantly become the topic of several brief conversations that spark.

"Ooooh her dress is ca-yuuute!" one girl squeals.

"Damn, look at those racks!" a guy says loudly.

"Her boobs are so fake," says a woman to her group of friends.

"Yeah, they look like water balloons," another in the group adds.

Fancy and Brittany enter Velvet and do their normal greeting of the staff and acquaintances they encounter as they make their way to their usual table in VIP. They arrive at the table to find Jaslyn waiting for them in a strapless red satin mini dress and red pumps.

"Dahling, you look fab," Brittany says in a phony British accent as they approach her.

"Daaaamn, my girls are bad!" Jaslyn replies. "Look at you two!" They all exchange hugs.

"Look at us *three*," Fancy corrects her.

"Nadine!" Brittany yells to the cocktail waitress as she walks by. "We need a bottle of Goose, sweetie!"

There is a sudden commotion at the door as bouncers try to clear a pathway through the crowd.

"Must be Aaron," Jaslyn says with a devilish grin.

"Uh-uh, Jas," Brittany says, "Fancy already called dibs on him, so don't you be trying to put the moves on him."

"May the best woman win," says Jaslyn, shrugging.

"Hey, I'm always up for a little friendly competition," Fancy replies.

Aaron Jameson and his large entourage are escorted through the crowd by security. Fancy, Brittany and Jaslyn, along with most of the other women in the VIP section, adjust their posture and touch up their lipstick as the group approaches. Aaron and his clique enter VIP and Fancy spots him as he walks past their table and is seated at the table next to theirs.

"He's fiiiine," Fancy whispers to her friends, "but he looks a lot taller on TV."

Nadine arrives with their vodka and mixers and they each have a shot before making their cocktails. Fancy mixes a little cranberry juice with a lot of vodka, creating a very strong concoction. She is nervous with Aaron sitting so close and wants to loosen up a bit.

After a few drinks the three ladies get up to dance. Fancy knows this is her chance to get Aaron to notice her. She moves seductively, gyrating her hips and swinging her hair as she runs her hands along her curves. She glances over at Aaron and it appears that he is looking in their direction, although she can't be sure at whom, since he is wearing sunglasses.

After several songs, the girls become too hot to continue dancing in the crowded VIP area and they sit down for a drink. Nadine approaches the table with a bottle of Moët & Chandon.

"It's from Aaron, ladies," she says. Fancy, Jaslyn and Brittany simultaneously look towards Aaron's table and smile. He nods and smiles back.

"Looks like he's been checking one of us out," Fancy says.

"Well I'm gonna go thank him," Jaslyn says, quickly jumping up and strutting over to Aaron's table before Fancy or Brittany can say a word. Fancy is shocked and turns to Brittany whose eyes and mouth are also wide with surprise.

"Unbelievable!" Fancy says.

Jaslyn stays at Aaron's table talking to him for a few minutes. Afterwards she returns and without a word begins pouring herself a glass of champagne.

"Well?" Fancy inquires.

"Well what?"

"What do you mean 'well what'? What did he say?"

"Nothing special. We just talked about regular stuff – that's all."

"That's crazy, Jas. You just run over there by yourself – you don't wait for anyone else to go – and then you wanna be all secretive and shit."

"The last time I checked we were all grown-ass, able-bodied women. If you wanted to come you could've gotten your ass up and came too. And I told you we didn't talk about anything major, alright, Fancy?"

"Fine then...whatever."

"Come the fuck on now!" Brittany exclaims, refilling each of their glasses. "We're here to have a good time. Let's get drunk and par-tay!"

The conversation is ended and Fancy downs her whole glass all at once. As they drink, the mood lightens and the tension between Fancy and Jaslyn dissipates. The party is raging. Fancy, Brittany and Jaslyn are having a great time dancing with each other atop the plush blue couches, until a bouncer comes over and taps Fancy on her hand.

"I guess they don't want us dancing on the sofa, guys," Fancy says to her friends as the bouncer helps her down.

"Aaron would like you to come to his table," he whispers in Fancy's ear. Keeping a straight face, Fancy simply nods to avoid appearing as excited as she is. When the bouncer walks away, she turns to her friends.

"Oh my God, Aaron wants me to come over there, guys."

"Well go on then," Jasyln replies, rolling her eyes. "You were ready to bite my damn head off over him earlier so what are you waiting for?"

"I'm nervous," says Fancy.

"Nervous about what?" Brittany asks. "Because he's famous? Trust me, he's just like any other guy. Ain't no need to be intimidated."

"You're right, Britt. Okay, here goes."

Fancy walks over to the table and Aaron motions for her to sit next to him.

"Hi," she says, sitting down and crossing her silky tan legs.

"Hey, beautiful. What's your name?

"Fancy."

"Fancy," he repeats. "A fancy name for a fancy girl."

"You enjoying your birthday?"

"I sure am. Especially now that you're here."

Fancy smiles and blushes.

Just then three waitresses appear, one carrying a birthday cake decorated with the 76ers' logo and several lighted candles, and two carrying bottles of champagne with sparklers. They begin singing "Happy Birthday" and everyone joins in. Fancy is blinded by the flashing cameras as what seems like hundreds of photos are taken, and she feels important sitting next to Aaron at the center of all the commotion. He blows out the candles and everyone applauds.

By the time the cake and champagne are gone, the music has stopped and the lights are on. The party has ended and people are leaving. The bartenders are sitting at the bar counting money. The club's floor, which, just several minutes ago, was hidden under a sea of dancing clubbers, now stands exposed and littered. The employees begin sweeping the floor and wiping off the tables.

"So where you headed now?" Aaron asks Fancy.

"With you," she bravely replies.

"I was hoping you'd say that."

Fancy and Aaron say goodbye to their friends before heading to his tinted black Bentley, which is parked right out front. They get in and Aaron speeds off down the street.

"So tell me some things about yourself, Ms. Fancy."

"What do you wanna know?"

"Start with the basics. That's always easy."

"Well, I'm 27, Puerto Rican, an Aries, no kids...ummm—"

"What do you do for a living?"

"Uh, I'm into...fashion.

"You're a fashion stylist?"

"Uh-huh."

"How'd you get into that?"

"Just networking, pretty much."

"That's cool. You do any designing or merchandising?"

"Yeah, sometimes."

Fancy is caught off guard by Aaron's questions. In her experience she has found that most men don't care to ask a lot of questions about her. They usually prefer to talk about themselves. While Fancy likes that Aaron is different in that way, she also hopes he doesn't ask any more questions she isn't prepared to answer. She exhales in relief when he turns the radio on.

As they listen to the smooth R&B track, Fancy stares in the passenger side mirror at the bright skyline of downtown Philadelphia. It becomes smaller and dimmer as they near the Ben Franklin Bridge, which will take them to Aaron's New Jersey home.

As the car approaches Aaron's estate, Fancy is left speechless by its breathtaking architecture. The tall black wrought iron gates open and he drives into the large stone roundabout and past the beautiful lighted fountain. He parks in front of the door and, in true gentleman fashion, dashes to open the passenger side door. They walk through the white oak double doors and Aaron takes her by the hand and leads her up the grand staircase to his bedroom.

With its king-sized bed, elegant décor and marble en suite bathroom, Aaron's bedroom resembles that of a five-star luxury hotel. The bed is covered with black and gold embroidered linens and almost a dozen matching decorative pillows. Oriental throw rugs adorn the glossy cherry wood floors. Framed Egyptian calligraphy hangs on the walls, along with a gold baroque clock and a large flat screen television.

"I'm gonna take a quick shower," he says, handing her the remote.

"K."

"There's drinks in the fridge if you get thirsty," he says, pointing to the mini refrigerator in the corner. "Feel free to get comfy and make yourself at home. Mi casa su casa."

"Thank you."

He closes the bathroom door and turns on the shower. Fancy gets up to check her hair and make-up in a large gold-framed mirror. She turns around, admiring the way her rotund backside looks in her dress.

She pictures Aaron standing naked in the shower, imagining how sexy his wet, glistening muscles must look as the water rolls off his toffee-colored skin. For a moment, she toys with the idea of joining him in the shower. The thought of it makes her smile. She shakes her head and attempts to dismiss the idea to no avail. The fantasy lingers in her mind.

Finally succumbing to her daydreams, Fancy decides there is no reason why she shouldn't be bold and make the first move. She slips out of her dress and quietly enters the steamy bathroom. She can see Aaron's blurred naked silhouette through the foggy glass shower walls. Her heart races with nervousness. *Too late to back out now*, she thinks to herself.

"Mind if I join you?" she asks, slipping in the back of the shower.

"Not at all," he replies, feasting his eyes on her curvy body as she slinks past him to the front of the shower. She drenches her long black hair and begins soaping herself.

"Let me give you a hand," Aaron says, gently moving her hair in front of her shoulder so he can wash her back. He moves closer and Fancy can feel his erection. She turns around to face him and runs her hands along his rock hard chest and abs. His strong hands explore the dimensions of her frame, eventually making their way to her full, supple breasts. Their lips meet in a deep, passionate kiss as Aaron's hands slide all over her smooth, slippery skin. He gently caresses her thighs and firmly cups her perfectly round backside. Fancy reaches for his thick, erect manhood, carefully guiding it to the threshold of her waiting love canal. She gasps with pleasure as he enters with a firm thrust. He lifts her up and she wraps her legs around him, moaning in ecstasy with each long stroke. She pulls him closer as her body writhes, pushing herself onto him with a fluid back and forth motion. With each thrust Aaron goes deeper and Fancy moans louder in rapture. It is a blissful climb to the peak of ecstasy, and when they finally arrive, they do so together, their bodies in perfect sync.

Fancy and Aaron are exhausted after their passionate love-making session. They towel each other off and climb into bed for some much needed shut-eye. Aaron lies in bed and silently gazes at Fancy for a moment.

"Goodnight, Fancy," he says, kissing her tenderly on her forehead before turning off the lamp. He holds her in his strong arms as he drifts off to sleep.

Despite her fatigue, a feeling of excitement keeps Fancy awake – excitement over the possibility of a future with Aaron. Being with him makes her feel special. *He could have picked any girl in the club*, she thinks to herself, *but he chose **me**.*

Chapter 8

Fancy awakens the next morning to the buzzing of Aaron's electric toothbrush. She sits up in bed just as he is emerging from the bathroom.

"Morning, beautiful," he says, smiling at her.

"Good morning," she smiles back.

"Did you sleep good?"

"Yes, I did."

"You hungry? I was thinking we could go grab some breakfast."

"I am, but...I don't really wanna go anywhere in my club clothes from last night. Why don't we stay in and I can cook something instead?"

"She cooks too!" Aaron exclaims. "You just might be perfect, Ms. Fancy."

Aaron doesn't have much food in his bachelor pad, but he has enough for Fancy to whip up a breakfast of home fries, scrambled eggs and bacon. She is not even half finished her food when she looks over and sees that Aaron has already devoured all of his.

"That was delicious, mama. Thanks."

"You're welcome. Glad you enjoyed it."

Aaron has to pack and get ready to leave for Orlando, so after breakfast they go get in the car so he can take her home.

"Where do you live?"

"I live at the Piazza, but I'm staying in the Northeast at my friend's while they renovate my building."

"Oh, okay. I was just at the Piazza yesterday afternoon. My homie stays there. He must be in a different building."

Forty-five minutes later they pull up in front of Brittany's house and prepare to say their goodbyes.

"Well, I enjoyed my evening and morning with you, Ms. Fancy. You made my birthday perfect. I hope you enjoyed yourself too."

"I did," she says, and the two share a warm hug and quick kiss before she exits the car.

"We'll link up again soon," he says. "Call me tonight, aight?"

"Okay. Bye Aaron."

"See you later, mama."

Brittany opens the door for Fancy and wastes no time getting the scoop.

"Wellllll?" she asks, eyes wide.

"Well..." Fancy begins, unable to stop smiling, "I really like him, Britt."

"Duh. Who wouldn't? He rich, famous and sexy as hell! Does he have a big dick?"

Fancy laughs loud and hard.

"I'll take that as a yes. I hope you put it on him, girl, cause you got a lot of competition. I hear he gets mad bitches."

Fancy's smile disappears. "Really? You think he's a player?"

"My friend Kim's cousin's stepsister used to fuck with him, and she said he likes to mess with a lot of different chicks. That's how most of these athletes are. They get pussy thrown at 'em all the time, so they just be hoin' around."

"You can't believe everything you hear, Britt. How many times have people spread rumors about us that aren't true? People just like to talk...that's all."

"Yeah, I guess. I'm just telling you what Kim told me."

"I don't know. He just doesn't seem like that. He seems...different."

Fancy finds Aaron to be unlike any of the other men she's dated. He is unique in so many ways: His chivalrous gestures; the way he shows a genuine interest in her; the gentleness of his caress; the way he tenderly kissed her on her forehead and held her close as they slept. No one had ever made her feel so special. She refuses to believe the things Brittany says about him. *Who the hell is her friend Kim's cousin's stepsister anyway?*

Chapter 9

Fancy and Aaron smile flirtatiously at one another from opposite sides of a table in a chic French restaurant.

"You're just mad because I whooped your ass in bowling," Fancy laughs.

"Nah, you're gonna have to give me a rematch," says Aaron. "I was off that day."

"Lame excuse."

"We should go to North Bowl next time."

"North Bowl?"

"Yeah you've probably been there a million times."

"I don't even know what it is."

"You've had to have seen it, Fancy. It's on the same block you live on."

"Ohhh, okay. I think I know what you mean."

"Yeah, the bowling place. There's no way you can live in the Piazza and not know it."

"I just forgot about it for a sec."

"Well, yeah, next time we gotta go there. They got the best buffalo wings."

After Aaron pays for dinner they head out to the car. During the ride home he inquires about when she will be returning to her apartment. Fancy has been at Brittany's for almost a week now and hasn't given much thought to when she'd be going home. She has been spending so much time with Aaron that the days have been quickly flying by. She's gotten quite comfortable staying with Brittany, who is an excellent hostess. And because Brittany secretly hates living alone, she also has not brought up the topic of Fancy leaving. Nonetheless, Fancy knows she should go home soon to avoid looking suspicious.

"I'm going home tomorrow."

"You want me to take you? I could pick you—"

"Nope," Fancy interrupts. "It's cool. Brittany's gonna take me."

"You sure? You know it's not a problem for me to come down and grab you, ma."

"Nah...really, it's okay. Thanks anyway, though."

For the first time, Fancy feels bad about lying to Aaron. He seems so honest and good-natured, and the more time she spends with him, the more she likes him. Although she was initially interested in him because of his money, she finds herself genuinely liking him for the person that he is. She considers coming clean to him, but wonders if he will still be interested in her if he knows who she really is. She decides she will tell him the truth – just not now.

It is the following morning and Fancy is dragging her bags up the cement steps leading to her apartment. She is breathing heavily after the trek from the bus stop and she can see her breath in

FANCY

the cold fall air. She inserts her key into the lock and is surprised to find it won't turn. She jiggles the key. Still no luck. Fancy examines the lock and notices that what was previously an old, rusty silver lock is now a shiny, new gold one. She is outraged to learn that the locks on her apartment have been changed.

"No fuckin' way," she says out loud, pulling her cell phone from her purse. "That bastard didn't even send a notice!" She locates the entry in her phone listed as "Asshole Joe" and presses the call button.

"Hello?" the voice on the other end of the call says with a Spanish accent.

"Why the fuck am I locked out of my apartment, Joe? I told you I'ma give you your damn money!"

"Oh, finally I hear from you. You had 'til the 15th. I sent three different notices – tres! – and I didn't hear nada."

"Whoa, whoa, whoa...what three notices? I didn't even get one!"

"I put them in the mail slot myself so don't even try it!"

Fancy remembers the pile of unopened mail sitting on the table in her apartment. *Fuck*.

"You're never home and your phone number always changes. How am I supposed to contact you? You're completely irresponsible! Always late with the rent. If you don't care then I don't care either!"

"Okay, look Joe...I'll have the money real soon. Couple of days...I swear! Just please come and open the damn door. I'm standing out here freezing."

"Too late for that. You had your last chance. I found a new renter – someone who knows how to be responsible."

"That's fucked up Joe! You can't give me one more chance?"

"Last time was one more chance, and the time before that. No more chances left, chica. You need to have your stuff out by next Friday so I can get the place ready for the new tenant. Call me when you're ready to get your things."

"Fuck you Joe! Pendejo cabrón!"

Angry and frustrated, Fancy sits on the cold cement steps and buries her face in her hands. She knows there is only one place she can go; and as much as she does not want to go there she knows she must, for it is her only option. Fancy lifts her head, letting out a long groan. She picks up her bags and begins the five block walk to her mother's house.

When Fancy arrives at Anna's she slowly and reluctantly ascends the stairs and inserts her key into the lock. *Please don't let her be home*, she thinks to herself. Although Anna has never turned Fancy away when she's needed a place to stay, she makes sure to nag and lecture her on a regular basis while she is there. Right now, Fancy is not in the mood for her mother's chiding. *Please don't let her be home*, she thinks to herself again, squeezing her eyes tight as she pushes the door open.

As soon as the door opens, the telenovela blaring from the TV lets Fancy know that her mother is, in fact, home.

"Hey, Mom."

"Bags? Ay díos mío, Fancy. Evicted again?"

"Again? This is the first time in a long time, Mom. I haven't been here in two years, okay?"

Fancy attempts to block out her mother's voice as she walks up the stairs to her room. However, a few words manage to make their way through: "irresponsible," "bum" and "grow up." She closes the door and sets her bags down, looking around at her old bedroom. Although her posters, teddy bears and other items from her adolescence had been boxed up and moved to the basement many years ago, the room still has the same rickety dresser and the same twin bed with the same old, squeaky mattress. The bed even has one of the same blankets on it that Fancy used as a kid: a white and lavender floral patchwork quilt.

Fancy's phone rings and she takes it out of her bag and sees that it is Aaron. She smiles and clears her throat before answering.

"Hey you."

"Hey mama. How you doin' today?"

"Great," she lies. "How about you?"

"I'm good. What you up to?"

"Not much, just in the crib straightening up a little."

"Good, I'm glad you're home 'cause I'm around your way. I had to pick up something from my man real quick. But since I'm here I figured I'd stop by and see you."

Fancy's heart feels like it has jumped up in her throat, and for a moment she is speechless.

"You still there, Fancy?"

"Yeah, it's just that, um...I'm not feeling too well."

"Stop playin', girl," Aaron laughs. "You just said you were great. I know you're cleaning or whatever, but you know I don't care if your place is a little junky. I just wanna see you."

"No, it's not that, Aaron. I'm really not feeling good right now."

"Well just come outside for a second, then."

"Aaron, really...it's...I got cramps."

Fancy's sure he'll drop it now. She knows men never want to discuss anything even remotely related to women's menstruation.

"Oh, uhhh...aight then. Just call me when you're feeling better."

"Okay. Talk to you later."

Chapter 10

The next day when Fancy picks up her phone to call Aaron, she discovers that her cell phone has been disconnected due to nonpayment. She uses the landline instead.

"Hello?"

"Hey Aaron. It's Fancy."

"Hey, mama. You feeling better?"

"Much better. But um, I messed up my phone. Dropped it in the bath tub."

"Where you calling me from now?"

"My mom's house."

"You still wanna link up tonight?

"Yeah. Where we going?"

"It's a surprise."

"Awww, come on. Give me a hint."

"Well, it's somewhere you've probably never been. You'll have fun, though."

"Wow, that was extremely helpful. How am I supposed to know how to dress, Aaron?"

"Just dress casually – jeans or whatever."

"Ummm, okay."

"So I'll pick you up at seven, aight?"

"Cool. See you then."

Fancy shivers as she waits at the bus stop. *This is absolutely ridiculous*, she thinks to herself. *I've got to tell him the truth – tonight*. She had planned on arriving early, but instead she is running late, so she gets off at the stop after the Piazza and walks back to ensure Aaron won't see her getting off the bus. She gets in the car and greets him with a kiss on the cheek.

"Hey, sweet thing. Where you coming from?"

Shit. He must've seen me walk up the street. "I just walked around the block while I was waiting."

"In the cold?"

"It isn't that bad out."

"It's freezing, Fancy."

"It's just a little windy. That's all."

"Where's there a T-Mobile store?"

"T-Mobile?"

"Yeah, your service is with them, right?"

"Yeah."

"Well where's the closest store? I can't have my girl not being able to reach me."

"Your girl?"

"Yeah, we might as well make it official. You diggin' me, right?"

"Yeah."

"And I'm feelin' you. So I don't see no reason why you shouldn't be my girl."

Fancy just smiles, but on the inside she is jumping up and down. *It's official! Aaron Jameson is my boyfriend! I have an amazing, handsome, sweet and caring man who also happens to be rich and famous.* Fancy thinks it is too good to be true.

Her excitement quells when she remembers that the woman Aaron wants to be in a relationship with is not the woman she really is. And while she wants to tell him the truth, she does not want to lose him.

After purchasing her new phone, they drive several miles before parking in front of a large indistinct brick building adjacent to the expressway. Aaron takes a duffle bag from the trunk and they walk hand-in-hand to the front door. There are no signs on the building and Fancy cannot figure out what the place might be – until they walk in the door. They are greeted by the sound of gunfire. Fancy is startled at first, but relaxes when she realizes they are at a firing range.

"Well, you were right. I've never been to a gun range before."

"Have you ever shot a gun?"

"Nope."

"You're gonna love it."

Aaron retrieves ammunition and protection for their eyes and ears at the front counter before taking a shiny black pistol from his bag. Fancy watches as Aaron shoots off several rounds. Hearing the continuous bang of the .45 ACP is exhilarating, and watching Aaron pump round after round into the target excites her. She can't wait to give it a try. When Aaron finally puts the gun down, Fancy quickly picks it up. It is heavy and warm to the touch.

"Whoa, mama. Hold on a sec," Aaron says, reaching into the duffle bag. "I got something else for you."

He pulls out a smaller handgun, a .357 revolver. Fancy grasps its handle, giving it a thorough examination.

"It's beautiful," she says, admiring the firearm's sleek silver finish.

"Exactly. Perfect for you."

Aaron shows her how to hold it and corrects her posture.

"Spread your legs a little. Hold it securely, but not too tight. Now brace this hand with your other hand. When aiming, always make sure you line up the sights. When you shoot, think about squeezing the trigger rather than pulling it back."

Fancy takes aim and slowly squeezes the trigger. BOOM! *Whoa*. The kick is more intense than she anticipates. Her hands jerk back and the bullet hits the top of the target. The sound of the gunshot echoes and smoke curls from the warm barrel. She fires the remaining four shots, each landing closer to the target's center.

"Damn," Aaron says with a surprised smirk. "Not bad for your first time."

After about an hour of shooting, Fancy and Aaron have dinner at a swanky Thai restaurant. When they have finished eating, she decides it's time to come clean and tell him the truth. Fancy knows Aaron is a good guy and hopes that although he may be upset about her lying, he will still feel the same about her once he knows who she really is. She takes a deep breath before she begins.

"Aaron, there's something I've got to tell you."

He looks into her eyes with concern.

"I'm not who you think I am."

"What do you mean?"

"I don't live at the Piazza. I live in the hood. And I'm not into fashion design. I don't even have a job. I lied...and I'm sorry."

They sit in silence as Fancy studies Aaron's puzzled expression. There is an awkward tension as Fancy awaits his response. Finally he speaks.

"Is that it?"

"Yeah."

Aaron laughs. "Whew. I thought you were about to tell me you were born a man or some shit."

"You're not mad?"

"No, I'm not mad. Fancy, I like you for *you*. I just don't understand why you'd lie about that stuff."

"I just wanted you to like me. Nobody else knows the truth. Not even my friends."

"You gotta be kidding me, Fancy. You can't keep putting on an act for people. That's no way to live your life. Be yourself. If people don't like you for who you really are, then fuck 'em!"

They laugh together. Fancy's excitement returns and she is joyful, her heart overflowing with pure happiness.

Chapter 11

Fancy's excitement over Aaron fails to subside. As the weeks go by her feelings for him grow deeper and stronger until she feels she has fallen in love with him. She professes her feelings for him and is ecstatic when he says he is in love with her too. She takes Aaron to meet her mother, who, unsurprisingly, is just as excited about him as Fancy is. Fancy is always happy when she is with Aaron. She spends as much time with him as possible. In fact, she spends so much time at his house and has so many of her things there, it looks as if she has moved in. However, she often finds herself wishing Aaron had more free time to spend with her. Lately he is extremely busy. When he's not out of town for an away game, he has either practice, an interview, a meeting or a home game. But Aaron makes sure Fancy is able to stay occupied while he is gone. He provides her with money and the unrestricted use of his credit card for her to shop and go out with. Transportation is not an issue. She simply calls for a limo whenever she needs to go somewhere and Aaron takes care of the bill. While she is at his house, Fancy tries to show her appreciation for his generosity as much as possible by straightening up between the housekeeper's visits and preparing her delicious dishes that Aaron so loves.

It is a Saturday evening and Fancy is making one of Aaron's favorites, roast beef. He has just gotten back from Los Angeles earlier and he is tired and jet-lagged. He tells her he is going to take a shower since he will have to leave for a meeting after dinner. Fancy slices some mushrooms and chops up an onion for the roast's gravy. She is making string beans to accompany it, and is torn between rice and mashed potatoes for the other side dish. She decides to go ask Aaron which he would prefer.

She walks up the stairs and into the bedroom. Aaron is still in the shower. As she nears the bathroom door, Aaron's phone vibrates on the dresser. She pauses for a moment then walks over to the dresser and picks up his phone. It is a text message from someone named Lisa. *Who the hell is Lisa?* Fancy knows she should not be looking in his phone but her curiosity will not allow her to walk away now. If the text had been from a John, a Steve, a Tyrone or any other male name, she would have immediately put the phone down and walked away without giving it a second thought. But knowing that it is from a woman, she simply has to see what it says. She opens the text message which reads, *Miss you, babe*. Unable to believe what she just read, she reads the words again, and then again. *That motherfucker!* Fancy shakes her head in disbelief. She notices that the area code is 310, which she's pretty sure is a Los Angeles area code. She is angry, sad, hurt and surprised by this discovery. Aaron seemed like such a great guy. More than anything she is extremely disappointed to find that he is no different from the rest. Her anger grows as she thinks about the broken trust. She wonders how he could be so deceitful. How could he just come home, look her in her eyes and tell her he loves her, knowing he had been with another woman? She finds herself wondering about the other woman, Lisa. *I bet she's pretty. Probably prettier than me, with a better body*. She pictures him kissing and caressing this Lisa. She imagines him making love to her, and afterwards, holding her tightly and kissing her tenderly on her forehead. Fancy's blood is boiling. Tears are streaming down her red cheeks. Aaron emerges from the bathroom to find Fancy standing in his bedroom, crying and holding his cell phone.

"Fancy, what's wrong?"

"Why don't you call your little bitch Lisa and ask her!" she yells, throwing the phone at him.

"Calm down, Fancy. You don't know what you're talking about."

Aaron reads the text message in his phone.

"Man, Lisa ain't nobody. She's just someone I know from back in the day – an old friend."

He reaches for Fancy's hand but she quickly yanks it away and storms to the other side of the room.

"Yeah, I bet she is. I bet you were running around with her the whole time you were out LA – probably fuckin' her too! After all, she misses you, right?"

"She's a friend from college, Fancy. I only saw her once while I was out there. We just got something to eat real quick since I was in town. It wasn't no date or nothin' like that. And hell no, I ain't fuckin' that girl!"

"Oh I find that very hard to believe. Friends don't call each other 'babe'!"

"That's just how she talks, man. She calls everybody 'babe'. I bet you know a bunch of chicks that call everyone 'babe', or 'sweetie' or 'hon'."

"Whatever. Fuck you, Aaron! It's over. I'm done!"

"Fuck me? No, fuck you, Fancy! I just got home and I'd think you'd be glad to see me, but instead you goin' through my fuckin' phone, accusing me of shit I didn't do. I told you she's an old friend from school and we just met up for lunch. I haven't seen that girl in years! You wanna make me out to be some fuckin' criminal because your ass is insecure, when I don't do shit but try to make you happy. So if you wanna make up stories in your head and come at me on some bullshit because you got trust issues, then FUCK YOU!"

Aaron goes back into the bathroom, slamming the door behind him.

Fancy sits on the bed dumbfounded, knowing neither what to do nor say. She considers the possibility that maybe Aaron is telling the truth. She has never seen him so angry, and he has never spoken to her like this before. He seems to be genuinely offended by her accusations. While she knows it is true that many women use pet names such as 'babe' loosely, she also thinks it seems highly unrealistic that someone would text a *friend* after just seeing them to tell them they miss them. Something about it just doesn't sit right with Fancy. Still, she has no concrete evidence that Aaron has been cheating. Finally she decides that perhaps she overreacted, and that while she won't totally rule out the possibility of him cheating, she's not going to assume the worst without knowing for certain.

    Fancy knocks lightly on the bathroom door before slowly opening it and sheepishly walking in. She gives Aaron a hug and apologizes for jumping to conclusions. He accepts her apology and she asks him if he wants rice or mashed potatoes with dinner.

Chapter 12

It is the following evening and Fancy is straightening up at Aaron's when she receives a phone call from Brittany.

"What's up, Britt?"

"Hey you. What you up to?"

"Nothin' much. You?"

"Chillin'. Me and Jas goin' to Velvet tonight. You should slide through. We ain't seen you in a minute."

"Yeah girl, it feels like ages since I've been out. Sounds like a plan, though. Usual time?"

"You know it. See ya later."

As she is hanging up the phone, Aaron walks in from practice.

"Hey, baby," she says, greeting him with a hug and kiss.

"Hey, mama. What you up to?"

"Just got off the phone with Britt. She wants to meet up at Velvet tonight. Wanna go?"

"Nah, I already told my man I'd swing through Pulse with him, so you go ahead and do ya thing with your girls."

"Okay then."

The driver picks Fancy up at 11:00 sharp. As she is on the way to Velvet, Jaslyn calls to say that some famous boxer is going to be at Club 101, so they'll be meeting there instead. Fancy notifies the driver of the change in destination and he adjusts his route accordingly.

Walking into the club, Fancy is anxious to see Brittany and Jaslyn. She can't wait to show off the new things Aaron bought her. They notice her new Balenciaga bag, sparkling diamond bracelet and fresh Christian Louboutin thigh boots as soon as they see her.

"Well would you look at this bitch!" Jaslyn says as Fancy approaches the table where she and Brittany are seated.

Brittany lets out a long, dramatic gasp when she sees Fancy's boots.

"The new Loubs! O-M-G they look soooo yummy. I could just eat them!"

"Well hello to y'all, too!" Fancy laughs.

"Damn girl, it's been a minute since we've seen you," says Jaslyn.

"Yeah 'cause she been too busy boo-lovin' with her baller," Brittany teases. "Bitch wanna act all new-new. Comin' up in here all icy and shit."

"Yes, girl. This bracelet," Jaslyn says, lifting Fancy's hand to admire her dazzling diamond bracelet. "Brilliant cut diamonds. Simply flawless. Where's the matching ring?"

"Ring?"

"Yeah girl, engagement ring."

"Ain't nobody talkin' about marriage just yet, Jas!"

"Well shit, you better start, because he's a hell of a catch."

"Yes! And nooooo prenup!" Brittany adds. They all laugh.

Suddenly, Jaslyn stops laughing. Her eyes are wide as saucers and steadily fixated on the club's front door. Fancy and Brittany notice her staring, and follow her gaze to see what has her in such shock. Walking through the door is a beautiful busty Middle Eastern-looking woman, escorted by none other than Aaron. His arm is around her waist, holding her close to him. She places her hand on his chest as they simultaneously laugh at something he says. They are smiling and having a great time, oblivious to the watchful eyes of Fancy and her friends.

Fancy's heart begins racing as she feels the rage of the previous night return, bubbling up inside her like a pot of boiling water.

"I don't believe this shit!" she says through clenched teeth.

"He is really trippin'," Jaslyn says.

"You wanna go fuck that bitch up, Fancy?" asks Brittany, springing up from her seat, "Because I'm wit it."

"Chill for a sec, Britt," Fancy says, trying not to show her anger.

The three continue to watch as Aaron and the woman are seated at a table at the other end of the VIP section, flirting and laughing all the while. Fancy can see that Aaron is very into her and it is obvious that they are more than friends. When he leans over and kisses the woman on her forehead, Fancy can no longer contain her rage. She leaps up and storms over to their table as tears flow from her eyes. Aaron does a double take when he looks up and sees an enraged Fancy marching toward him.

"Didn't expect to see me here, huh motherfucker? Well you ain't gotta worry about seeing me anywhere anymore. Have fun running around with all your lil' hos, you cheatin' ass pussy!"

And with that she rips the diamond bracelet off her wrist and throws it in his face before storming out of the club.

Fancy has the driver take her to her mother's house, where she quietly slips in the front door, up the stairs, out of her clothes and into bed. She tightly hugs her pillow as she sobs quietly, thinking about the act of betrayal she just witnessed. Her broken heart is heavy with sorrow. She thinks about how happy she had been to have finally found a man she genuinely loved – one she thought loved her as well. It pained her greatly to watch him interacting with the woman as affectionately and as playfully as he had with her. Every gesture was familiar. She recognized the seemingly caring and gentle way in which he touched the woman, for it was the same way he had touched her. It infuriated her to watch him gaze attentively into her eyes, absorbing her every word, just as he had done with her. But she was most dismayed to see he was shameless enough to mimic even the tender forehead kiss that she had so adored. *He didn't even bother to say anything, or to come after me*, Fancy realizes. She finds herself beginning to wonder whether Aaron had ever really loved her at all. Perhaps it had all been an act from the very beginning – a scripted, well-rehearsed performance from an actor just as skilled as her.

Chapter 13

Fancy wakes up at 11:43 AM with a pounding headache. She looks in the mirror at her mascara-stained face, which she hadn't even bothered to wash before getting in bed. She goes to the bathroom, brushes her teeth and washes away the dried up tears and make-up before heading downstairs. She finds her mother in the kitchen making avena.

"Morning, Mom."

"What's wrong with you? You look like a bus hit you."

"Bad night."

"Aaron out of town?"

"No. We broke up. I won't be seeing him anymore."

"Damn, Fancy. How'd you mess that up? He's a good guy."

"Me? I didn't do anything. And he's not a good guy. He's a lying, two-faced cheater."

"What man isn't? You better make up with him. You stay with Aaron and you'll be set for the rest of your life. You see how good he takes care of you; you need that. You need a man that's gonna provide for you since you can't provide for yourself."

Anna has struck a nerve.

"You think I'll be happy alone in a big mansion while my man runs around on me?" she yells. "What kind of life is that?"

"A life of stability, Fancy! You like having all these expensive clothes and shoes. How do you expect to live that lifestyle?"

"I don't know," Fancy says, sitting down to calm herself. "Maybe that lifestyle ain't for me. Maybe I should go to college or something."

Anna bursts out in a roaring laugh, upsetting Fancy again.

"I don't find anything funny about that, Mom! I guess you forgot how smart all my teachers used to say I was. I got straight A's on every report card. But you never cared about that."

Anna continues to laugh and Fancy grows angrier.

"How come you've never been supportive of me getting an education? The only thing you've ever encouraged me to do is be a gold digger! I'm done with that. I don't wanna be that person no more. I don't wanna have to depend on a man to survive. I don't wanna end up like YOU!"

Anna, who is no longer laughing, is now angry and yelling defensively.

"This ain't about me, Fancy! This is about you needing to get your life together! What are you doing with yourself? All you wanna do is party, party, party. You're 27 years old and you can't even keep a roof over your head! A man comes along that can change that and somehow you manage to mess that up!"

Fancy realizes that arguing with her mother is a pointless, losing battle.

"You just don't get it," she says, shaking her head, "and you never will."

She goes back upstairs to her room, accepting that she and her mother will never see eye to eye.

Fancy picks up her phone to see three missed calls and a text message from Aaron: *Baby, I'm sorry about last night. I fucked up. Give me a chance to fix it. Call me ASAP. We can work this out. I love you.*

Without hesitation she deletes the text message and dials a number that is not listed in her phone's address book. It is a number she knows by heart.

"Whassup, Fancy?" the raspy voice on the other end asks, pleasantly surprised.

"Hey Shawn."

Over the years Fancy has always kept in touch with Shawn. Although they don't talk often, Shawn is the only person that Fancy considers a real friend. Fancy knows she can depend on Shawn whenever she is down and in need of someone to talk to. Shawn is always there with an open ear and a natural ability to console and comfort her.

Likewise, whenever Fancy calls, Shawn knows she must prepare to offer her a shoulder to cry on. Shawn wishes Fancy wouldn't only call when she is troubled, but nonetheless, she is always glad to hear from her old friend. In a way, Shawn feels partially responsible for Fancy becoming the person she's turned out to be. So, like a good parent who is there to comfort and guide her wayward child, Shawn is always there for Fancy.

"It's been a minute," Shawn says. "How you doin'?"

"I'm aight."

"You ain't aight. I can hear in your voice that something's up. Where you at? I'll come scoop you and we can rap about it."

"I'm at my mom's."

"Be there in a half."

Exactly 30 minutes later Shawn pulls up in a dark blue 1988 Cutlass Supreme. She honks the horn, signaling for Fancy to come outside. Fancy recognizes the horn when she hears it; she could recognize it anywhere.

"Oh my God, the Shawn-mobile! I cannot believe you still have that car, Shawn."

"Yup, I'ma ride her 'til her wheels fall off."

Fancy and Shawn pick up some Chinese food and go to Shawn's apartment, where Fancy shares the details about the events that unfolded the night before.

"Damn, dude gon' have me rootin' against the Sixers," Shawn says afterwards. "Fuck him, man. You already know you deserve better than that."

"I wish somebody would tell my mom that. She thinks I'd be better off staying with him."

"Your mom is a different woman than you are. She's trying to live vicariously through you. She wants you to do what she would do, but you're not her."

"That's for damn sure. She's so cold and insensitive, and unsupportive as fuck. I mentioned going to college and don't you know this bitch laughed in my fuckin' face?"

Shawn shakes her head.

"Well you know not to pay her no mind. That's just how she is. But on some real shit that's probably one of the best ideas you've ever had."

"College?"

"Hell yeah. You know under all this Gucci and shit you're still a nerd. What would you major in?"

Fancy shrugs.

"Well what do you think you'd wanna do as a profession?"

"I don't know. Maybe nursing. It's good money and I'd be helping people."

"Yeah, I can see you doing that. Well look, I don't know shit about college or student loans or none of that stuff, but my homeboy Dame goes to Community, and he can definitely help you out. I'll hit him up and see when he can come over and show you all that shit on the computer."

Chapter 14

Shawn's friend Damon has a wealth of information to share, and turns out to be instrumental in assisting Fancy throughout the college admission process. He helps her apply for and ultimately get accepted to the Community College of Philadelphia's nursing program, as well as secure financial aid.

It is December and the new semester will begin in about a month. Fancy is nervous about starting college. Sure, she had always been a good student in school, but that was years ago and college is a whole new ball game.

"You'll do fine," Shawn assures her. "You know your ass is a brainiac. Stop worrying...you got this."

Fancy smiles at Shawn. Her words calm her fears for the time being.

"Thanks Shawn," Fancy begins, "for everything. I appreciate you being such a good friend. You've really helped me stay sane and keep my mind off that clown Aaron."

Fancy has been spending a great deal of time at Shawn's lately, working with Damon and often spending the night. Being around Shawn makes her realize how much she's missed her, and how lucky she is to have had her as a friend for so long. Fancy is regretful about not keeping in touch with Shawn the way she should have. She realizes she's been so busy gallivanting with Brittany and Jaslyn, that she has been totally neglecting her one true friend. Shawn has always cared for Fancy. In high school they were inseparable, and even back then Shawn always had Fancy's back.

Like the time they had gone to a mall on the outskirts of the city to shoplift. It was Fancy's first time boosting after several weeks under Shawn's tutelage. Fancy was eager to finally prove herself after many outings spent observing as Shawn "worked."

The first time Fancy accompanied her on a shoplifting excursion, Shawn explained her methods as she went along.

"The first thing you do is locate the cameras," Shawn said as they entered a department store. Fancy looked up toward the ceiling.

"No! You gotta be subtle about it. You can't be all obvious with it or you'll draw attention to yourself."

"Alright, damn...my bad."

"There's one in that corner over there, one behind us to the right and one directly above us. Now as long as you know where the cameras are pointed, you're good. When your back is to a camera it can't get a visual what you're hands are doing in front of you. If the cameras are in front of you, go behind shit like shelves or clothing racks. You gotta be natural about it though so you don't look suspicious. And be quick – never linger."

"Okay, got it."

"Now let's go over here." They walked over to the women's intimate apparel section. "You see how all these people are over here? This is a good area to work in."

"Because security can't be watching everybody at the same time?

"No, it ain't about that. If you the only nigga – or, in your case, spic - in the bunch, they ain't gonna be worried about watching the whities anyway. They gonna be focusing on you and trust me, they'll be watchin' yo' ass like a hawk. But this is a good spot because you can use these people as a shield. You can get behind 'em so the cameras can't see what you're doing."

"Oh, okay."

"Now it's certain people you gotta watch out for."

"Employees?"

"Well yeah, of course. But there's others too. Most of these motherfuckas shoppin' are so caught up in what they're doing they won't even notice you. But look around. Is there anyone that looks out of place?"

"No, not to me."

"So you're telling me that grown ass man right there looking at women's drawers doesn't strike you as odd?"

"He could be shopping for his wife. Or maybe he just likes women's panties." Fancy laughs and Shawn shakes her head.

"Or maybe he's a secret shopper."

"What's a secret shopper?"

"Someone that gets paid to walk around stores and blend in so they can catch yo' ass stealin'."

"Ohhh."

"Yeah. Watch out for them."

After several more lessons and many times tagging along on Shawn's mall outings, Fancy felt that she was finally ready to try her hand at shoplifting. They decided to go to the same suburban mall department store where Shawn had given Fancy her initial training. Once inside the store she was a bundle of nerves. Still, she wanted to prove to herself and to Shawn that she could do it. Keeping Shawn's teachings in mind, she stuffed her messenger bag with all the jewelry and lingerie it could hold, while Shawn filled hers with tops and jeans. She was mindful of all the cameras – at least she thought she was. But when they walked out of the store a mall security guard was waiting for them.

"Excuse me," he said, holding a walkie-talkie at his side, "I need you two to come with me."

Fancy, shocked and scared, just stood there, frozen and unable to speak.

"What for?" Shawn asked.

"You have some items in your bags that you didn't pay for."

Shawn began walking back inside the store. Fancy did as well and the security guard followed. Suddenly, Shawn turned and darted back out of the store.

"Come and get me, you punk ass rent-a-cop!" she yelled at the security guard, who quickly took off after her. Instead of turning down the corridor that led to the exit, Shawn ran straight down the middle of the mall. Then she shouted back, "Run, Fancy, run! Get outta here, now!"

Fancy, running as fast as she could, made a right down the corridor, ran out the door and didn't stop running until she was four blocks from the mall.

The security guard eventually caught up with Shawn. She was arrested and placed on probation, in addition to the fines and community service she was given.

When Fancy thanked Shawn, she replied, "It's nothing. I'm the one that got you into that mess anyway. You ain't got no business boosting. You're a good girl."

It was a close call. Fancy never shoplifted again. And she always appreciated Shawn's helping her out of that jam.

Today, years later, Shawn still remains in her corner. Fancy vows to keep in close contact with her good friend.

"I'm sorry I've been so out of touch the past few months," she tells Shawn. "From now on, I'ma make sure I do better."

Chapter 15

By the time the beginning of the semester rolls around, Fancy is too busy to be nervous. On her first day she roams around the school's campus trying to locate her classes. She is shocked to learn the number of books she must buy – some classes require two or three different books. When she goes to purchase them, the bookstore is a crowded, chaotic mess. Mobs of students pack the store and Fancy is there for well over an hour tracking down her textbooks and waiting in the seemingly endless line. She is appalled at how expensive some of the books are, and she ends up not having enough money to buy all the ones she needs. Fancy is exhausted when she finally gets home, but now, instead of being nervous, she is excited about her future and proud to call herself a college student.

As the weeks go by, school remains Fancy's top priority. Rather than socializing and making friends, she keeps to herself in class. She listens intently to her professors and diligently takes notes. Finding much of the work challenging, she studies hard to better grasp the material. Even on the weekends she can be found buried in her books.

"I'm really proud of you," Shawn says to Fancy one night as she is studying for a political science test.

"Proud of me?" asks Fancy, looking up from her textbook. "For what?"

"For seeing this college shit through and staying focused. No partying, no bullshitting. You're always in the books. It's like you made a total 360. That's what's up."

"Aw, thanks Shawn. I'm trying. This test, though...I just don't know if I can do it. It's tomorrow and even though I've been studying my ass off, I still don't get this stuff."

"Here you go again. Always acting like you don't understand. And watch, tomorrow you'll go right in there and get an A."

"I doubt that."

Fancy stays up late studying for the test, finally turning in at 3:30 AM. She is awakened by her alarm only four hours later, exhausted and with a stomach ache that she figures is due to anxiety over the test. She doesn't have an appetite for breakfast, so she settles for a cup of coffee, which she hopes will keep her awake and alert for the test. She soon finds herself regretting the coffee as the liquid is tossed around her empty stomach during the bumpy bus ride to campus. Fancy is glad the test is in her first class, and plans to go home and rest immediately after it. Still, her stomach hurts so bad she hopes she can make it through the test.

Fancy sweats as she tries to concentrate on the questions in front of her instead of on the persistent, churning pain in her lower abdomen. The sensation intensifies and she lays her head on the cold desk, hoping it will pass. Then she begins to get nauseous. Her mouth starts to water and she can feel the coffee rising up her esophagus as she darts to the bathroom. When she returns to the classroom, she is met with dozens of pairs of curious eyes. She walks back to her seat and continues working on her test. Several minutes later, her mouth begins watering again and she runs back to the bathroom. This time when she returns, her professor is waiting for her outside the classroom door.

"Go home, Ms. Alvarez," the thin, balding man says, looking at Fancy over the rims of his thick glasses. "You're obviously ill. You can make the test up later."

"Thanks, Mr. Wolfe."

Within a couple of hours the pain has gotten much less intense, although a dull, achy feeling remains. Fancy still doesn't have much of an appetite and she quickly realizes that what she had attributed to anxiety and coffee on an empty stomach is obviously some sort of stomach virus.

Over the next few days, the scenario plays out similarly; the pain is at its worst early in the day, she vomits a few times and by the end of the day she's left with a dull, nagging pain.

After missing an entire week of classes due to her sickness, Fancy decides to see a doctor. She doesn't have health insurance, so she goes to the free clinic. Following a long wait in the crowded waiting room, she is called in to be seen.

"Hello, Ms. Alvarez," says the doctor, a petite Indian woman with glasses and a long, thick braid. "I'm Dr. Patel. What brings you in today?"

"I think I have a stomach virus. My stomach hurts all the time, but the pain is the worst in the morning," Fancy explains.

"How long have you had these symptoms?"

"It's been about a week now."

"Any vomiting?"

"Yes, but usually only early in the day, then it passes."

"Diarrhea?"

"No."

"Change in appetite?"

"Yeah, my appetite hasn't been too good. I've been eating mostly fruit and bread."

"What's the date of the first day of your last period?"

"Ummm, I don't know. I guess like a month or so ago. It's always been irregular though."

"Ms. Alvarez, I don't think you have a stomach virus."

Chapter 16

BOOM, BOOM, BOOM!

"Who the fuck is it?!"

"It's me! Open up."

"Damn, Fancy!" Shawn says, swinging her front door open. "You knockin' like you the cops or some shit. You cool?"

"I'm pregnant."

"What? For real?"

"Yeah, for real. I'm three months already! Due in July."

"Ohhh shit."

Shawn didn't know whether to congratulate Fancy or not, as Fancy stood at her front door staring back at her with desperate eyes.

"Come inside, Fancy. You want some water or something?"

"What am I gonna do, Shawn?"

"Well, what do you feel like you wanna do?"

"I don't know. I don't like the idea of getting an abortion, but I ain't ready for a baby. I mean, I want kids, but not like this. I wanna be married and do it right."

"Man, who's to say what's right? Everything happens for a reason. Maybe you're just supposed to have a baby now. I think you'd make a great mother."

"I don't know. I just can't believe I'm actually pregnant."

"You tell Aaron yet?"

"No. I so do *not* wanna call him."

"Well, you gotta let him know he's about to be a daddy. You might as well get it over with now. No point in waiting."

"I guess you're right."

Fancy hesitantly takes her phone from her purse and dials Aaron's number but nervously hangs up after the first ring. After several minutes of prodding and encouragement from Shawn, she reluctantly redials.

"Hello?"

"Aaron, it's Fancy."

"Hey mama. I knew you'd start missin' me eventually."

"Please. Don't flatter yourself. That is *not* why I'm calling."

"Then why? You already got all your stuff from over here."

"I...I'm...I'm pregnant."

"Ummm okay. I don't know what you tellin' me for, 'cause it ain't mine."

"Stop fuckin' playing with me, Aaron. I don't need this shit right now!"

"Ain't nobody playin'. I see what you're trying to pull, but it ain't gonna work. You ain't the first groupie ho to pop up claiming to be pregnant by me, and I'm sure you won't be the last."

"Groupie ho?! You're really gonna sit there and try to play me like I was just some random bitch to you? Who the fuck you frontin' for?!"

"Look, bitch, don't call my fuckin' phone no more. Good luck with your baby and have a nice life."

Fancy is in tears before Aaron hangs up the phone. She cries loudly, sobbing uncontrollably with her face buried in her hands. Shawn rubs her back, attempting to comfort her, but Fancy needs to cry; and cry she does, long and hard.

When Fancy tells her mother about the pregnancy, Anna acts as if Fancy has won the lottery.

"Oh, Fancy, you've finally done something right," she says. "Think of the child support checks!"

Anna is just being her regular, money-minded self. She cannot understand why her daughter is upset.

"So what if he doesn't wanna stick around? You don't need him. You'll have his money to support you and the baby."

"All you can think about is money! What about the fact that my child will grow up without a father?"

"Open your eyes, Fancy. Look how many women raise their children by themselves these days. I did it. Lots of other women are doing it. You'll do it, too, and guess what – you'll survive."

Fancy wondered if perhaps the reason she, herself, ended up so misguided is because she never had her father in her life. Would she have become a different person if he had been there?

Fancy quickly regrets mentioning the pregnancy to her mother. *That was pointless. I knew what she'd say before she even opened her mouth.*

Chapter 17

One quiet evening Fancy lies on the couch of her friend/therapist Shawn, wallowing in self-pity. She has fallen into a deep depression. There are various factors contributing to her stress, all of them related to her unexpected pregnancy. She is disappointed over Aaron's reaction to the pregnancy; saddened by the thought of her unborn child growing up fatherless; discouraged and disappointed because she has completely abandoned college and her hopes of becoming a nurse; and overall pessimistic about her future and her life. Shawn looks at Fancy, whose worries are written all over her face, and decides to try to cheer her up with a silly joke.

"So a horse walks into a bar," Shawn begins, "and the bartender says 'Why the long face?'"

"Okay..." says Fancy, awaiting the rest of the joke.

"That's it."

"That's the whole joke?"

"Yeah, don't you get it? He said 'Why the long face?' It's a horse. Of course it's gonna have a long face."

The two friends share a laugh. Mission accomplished. Shawn is glad to see Fancy's frown turn into a smile, even if only for a moment.

The corny joke is a small gesture, but an appreciated one, nonetheless. Fancy is happy to have Shawn to help her cope with her situation. She can always count on Shawn's silly stories and jokes to provide a much-needed distraction from the depressing thoughts clouding her mind. Shawn is Fancy's only refuge from her bleak reality.

Shawn is still laughing when Fancy rises from the couch and walks over to the chair where she's sitting. She gently lowers herself onto Shawn's lap and lovingly strokes her cheek. Gazing deep into Shawn's eyes, Fancy leans in and plants a soft kiss on her lips, and then another, and another, followed by a longer, deeper kiss. This isn't the first time the two have locked lips. Fancy and Shawn had kissed once back in high school.

It was Fancy's 17th birthday and Shawn had invited her to come over to her house that evening. As Fancy stood at Shawn's front door waiting for her to open it, she wondered what Shawn had in store for her.

"Hey, birthday girl," Shawn said opening the door.

"That's me," sung Fancy.

"Come on in. I got a surprise for you."

"Oooh, can't wait to see what it is."

"Ta-daaaa!" Shawn said, extending her arm toward the dining room table with the enthusiasm of a game show host presenting the grand prize. "I made you dinner."

On the table sat a pair of lit candles and two plates of baked salmon, collard greens, mashed potatoes and cornbread.

"Awww thanks, Shawn! It looks delicious. I'm starving too. Come on, let's grub!"

Dinner was every bit as tasty as it looked.

"I had no idea you were such a good cook," Fancy said after dinner. "I mean I know you can fry some good ass chicken, but this...this is *all that*!"

"Yeah man, those ain't no canned collard greens either. And those mashed potatoes are from scratch."

"I can tell. They're bangin! How'd you learn how to cook like this?"

"Man, you see my mom's like 500 pounds. How the hell you think I learned?"

Fancy laughed so hard she almost choked on her food.

"You're a mess, Shawn."

"Oh I almost forgot..."

Shawn disappeared into the kitchen and came back out carrying a round birthday cake and singing "Happy Birthday." The cake was red velvet with cream cheese icing that read *Hapy Birthday Fancy* in pink letters. There were 17 pink and white striped candles on top of it and when Shawn finished singing, Fancy made a wish and blew them out.

"Did you make this yourself too?" she asked Shawn.

"Of course. You think 'happy' would be spelled wrong if it came from the bakery?"

"I didn't even notice," Fancy laughed.

"One more thing," Shawn said, pulling a small grey box with a shiny red bow on it from her pocket and sliding it across the table to Fancy.

Fancy opened the box to find a beautiful gold heart locket inside.

"Oh my God, Shawn. This is beautiful. I love it."

"Open it."

When Fancy opened the locket she saw that the inside was engraved. One side said *Fancy* and the other said *Maribel*.

"Because even though you're my Fancy," Shawn said, "I want you to remember to always stay true to Maribel – stay true to yourself, because no matter what you're wearing or what you got, you're still a beautiful person, inside and out."

"Thank you, Shawn."

Fancy walked over to Shawn with wide, outstretched arms. She wrapped them firmly around Shawn who returned the hug, squeezing tightly. They shared a long, warm embrace. Then Shawn put her mouth on Fancy's and, for a brief moment, they locked lips until Fancy pulled away, looking and feeling awkwardly embarrassed.

"I'm sorry," Shawn said. "It's just that I've liked you for a while and...well, I'm sorry if I made you uncomfortable."

"It's okay. I like you too, Shawn, but not like that. You're like my best friend. And I don't wanna mess that up."

They had not kissed again since then – until now. The kiss certainly takes Shawn by surprise. Afterwards she opens her mouth to speak, but no words come out. Fancy doesn't speak either. She just sits there on Shawn's lap and quietly lays her head on Shawn's shoulder. Shawn wraps her arms around Fancy and together they sit contently. Fancy likes being held close by Shawn. It makes her feel loved and cared for, and although she had been wrong about Aaron and about many others in the past, with Shawn she knows it's real.

Chapter 18

It is several days later, on a Saturday night, when Shawn suggests that she and Fancy go out.

"It'll do you good to get out the house," she says.

"But I can't even drink," Fancy argues.

"You ain't gotta drink just because you're going out. You can still dance. You better have fun now, before that belly gets big."

"Good point. Where ya wanna go?"

"I know you like that spot Velvet. Let's go there. I've never been."

"Okay. I gotta get something to wear from my mom's."

"I'll get dressed first, then we can stop by there and head straight to the club after."

About 25 minutes later, Shawn emerges from her room wearing dark blue jeans, black suede loafers and a black button up shirt with neon orange, turquoise and lime green vertical stripes.

"Okay, let's go," she says, grabbing her keys from the table.

"Is that what you're wearing?" Fancy asks, staring at Shawn's shirt.

"Yeah, you like it?"

"Well, it's kind of..."

"Kind of what?"

"Kind of...loud."

"Loud?"

"It's just that Velvet is like an upscale kind of place."

"Just forget it then. I guess I ain't *upscale* enough for your type of places."

"Noooo, don't get offended. I just don't want you to feel uncomfortable."

"No Fancy, you just don't want *you* to feel uncomfortable. I guess my *loud* shirt will embarrass you in front of all those *upscale* people."

Shawn shakes her head.

"You know it ain't even like that," Fancy says, wrapping her arms around Shawn's neck and planting a kiss on her lips. "Stop trippin'."

"Aight," Shawn says, letting it go. "You go in there and find me something *upscale* to wear then."

Fancy disappears into Shawn's room and comes back a minute later with a plain dark gray dress shirt. Shawn changes her shirt and they leave the apartment arm in arm.

After walking through the front door of her mother's to find the house empty, Fancy exhales a sigh of relief. She is grateful any time she is spared the ordeal of having to converse with Anna. She quickly changes from her tunic and leggings into a short brown sweater dress and bronze ankle boots. She throws on a little make-up then she and Shawn are on their way.

When they arrive, Shawn pulls up directly in front of the club.

"What are you doing?" Fancy asks.

"What does it look like I'm doing, Fancy? I'm valeting the car."

"Are you serious? You're really gonna valet the Shawn-mobile?"

"Why wouldn't I?"

"Come on, Shawn. I know you love your car, but it's kind of, you know...we can just park in a lot."

Shawn slams her foot on the gas pedal and the tires screech loudly as the car peels off.

"Damn, slow down, Shawn. I want to live to have this baby," Fancy says. "Hey, you just passed the lot."

"Fuck the club, Fancy! I'm taking my ass the hell home."

"Why? We got dressed and came all the way down here already."

"Obviously I ain't good enough to be seen with you. My clothes are too loud; you don't wanna be seen gettin' out my shitty car. You're so fuckin' concerned with what everyone is gonna think of you – what everyone is gonna say. Well ya know what? One of these days you're gonna realize that none of these bougie motherfuckers really give a shit about you! But by that time it'll be too fuckin' late 'cause you'll already have pushed away everyone that actually does!"

Fancy silently stares out the window processing what Shawn just said. They don't exchange any more words for the remainder of the ride.

When they pull up in front of her mother's house, Fancy does not get out of the car. Instead, she sits there next to Shawn in silence searching for something to say. She wants to tell Shawn that everything she said was right; that she is her only true friend, and that she doesn't want to lose her. She wants to apologize for being so insensitive and for hurting Shawn's feelings. She wants to promise her she'll never act like that again. She wants them to hug and for Shawn to smile and tell her she forgives her. But all Fancy says is "I'm sorry" and Shawn neither acknowledges nor responds to Fancy's brief apology. Fancy finally gets out and Shawn speeds off as soon as the car door closes. Fancy watches the Shawn-mobile's taillights vanish up the street as the screeching of its tires simultaneously fades.

Chapter 19

Fancy doesn't feel right about the events that transpired or how the night ends. Before going to bed she decides that tomorrow she will give Shawn a proper apology and say all that is on her mind. But after calling numerous times the next day, Fancy is unable to reach Shawn. Her phone just rings repeatedly and then the voicemail comes on. Although it is unlike Shawn to hold a grudge, Fancy figures she must still be upset. She isn't going to let another day end without things being made right between them. She puts on her black wool pea coat and makes the seven-block trek to Shawn's apartment.

Fancy knocks on the door and is surprised when it cracks open to reveal an unexpected face. Although it has aged significantly and Fancy hasn't seen the face in years, she recognizes it immediately.

"Ms. Mercer?"

The face is Shawn's mother's, and as she opens the door wider to let her in, Fancy notices it is sorrowful and tear-stained. Fancy can tell from her pained expression that something is not right.

"What's wrong?" she asks fearfully. "Where's Shawn?"

Vanna B.

"My baby," Shawn's mother says, her throaty voice cracking as she unsuccessfully attempts to fight back tears. "My baby is dead!"

"No," Fancy says, shaking her head as her eyes fill with tears. "No, it can't be true. I was just with her!"

"Last night," Ms. Mercer sobs, "a drunk...a goddamned drunk son-of-a-bitch ran his truck into her car! My baby! My poor baby!"

Ms. Mercer collapses onto the floor. Fancy sits down next to her and hugs her tightly. Together they sit there on the floor by the door and share a long, hard cry.

The news has hit Fancy like a knife in the back – suddenly and unexpectedly – with the blade penetrating her heart, leaving it broken and bleeding out as quickly as the tears bleeding from her eyes. She wishes Ms. Mercer's cry would turn into a laugh and that she would tell Fancy that it was all a joke and that Shawn is alive and well. But she knows that is not going to happen.

After several minutes, Fancy helps Ms. Mercer up from the floor and walks her to the couch. She takes some tissues from the box on the coffee table and hands them to Ms. Mercer before taking a couple for herself. They sit on the couch in silence, wiping their eyes and noses. Finally Shawn's mother speaks.

"I would have called you but I didn't have your number."

"That's alright, Ms. Mercer. Is there anything I can do?"

"Well, I'm gonna have to turn in photos of Shawna to the funeral director. I only have a few. Do you have any they could use?"

Fancy nods. "I'll bring them by tomorrow."

"Thank you."

"I just can't believe this, Ms. Mercer. I can't believe she's gone. I was just with her and now we're talking about her funeral."

Fancy's voice cracks as her eyes well up again. She blinks and as the tears spill out she quickly catches them with a tissue.

After a while Ms. Mercer says she has to go and offers Fancy a ride home, which she accepts. As they pull up outside her mother's house, Fancy unbuckles her seatbelt.

"Thank you for the ride, Ms. Mercer. I'm so sorry about Shawn. Let me know if you need anything, okay? Anything at all."

"Thank you. I appreciate it."

"I'll bring the pictures by tomorrow morning."

Fancy gets out of the car and closes the door. She is walking up the steps when Ms. Mercer lowers the car window.

"Fancy..."

"Yes?"

"Would you say a few words about Shawna at the funeral? I know I won't be able to stand up there and do it. And nobody knew her as well as you did."

Fancy nods.

Ms. Mercer pulls off and Fancy walks into the house to find her mother snuggled up on the couch with an unfamiliar man. The man is sporting greasy shoulder-length hair, a five o'clock shadow and a round beer belly, which is poking out from underneath the white tank top he is wearing with his unbuttoned blue guayabera.

"Come here, Fancy," Anna says. "I wanna introduce you to Rafael."

"Hi Rafael," Fancy says dryly, walking past them into the dining room.

"Fancy, come over here and meet him. You're being rude."

"I'm not trying to be rude, but it's been a really long and stressful day. Shawn died."

"Oh no. I'm sorry to hear that. What happened?"

"I don't wanna talk about it right now. I really just wanna be alone."

Fancy opens the basement door and walks down the stairs. It is a disorganized hodgepodge of dusty furniture and old exercise equipment, with bags of outdated clothing and mountains of tattered boxes everywhere. She scans the cluttered cellar, searching for a powder pink hatbox with a ballerina on it, but sees no sign of it. She looks in the closets as well as under and behind things, but she still doesn't find the box. Fancy begins opening boxes, hoping their contents will provide a clue as to where the hatbox might be. The first box she looks in contains Christmas decorations, followed by a box of shoes and one with dishes in it. Then she finds a box of some of her old stuffed toys.

"Miss Pinky!" she exclaims, holding up a beat-up pink toy dog. It's been years since Fancy has seen her beloved stuffed poodle. Giggles, a fuzzy blue gorilla, is also in the box, along with a few Barbie dolls and Cabbage Patch Kids. Then Fancy comes across an old toy that instantly brings back her sadness. It is Chico, a big plush frog holding a heart that says "Get Well Soon." Shawn had given it to her when she was hospitalized with the flu, and seeing it brings her back to the cold reality that she will never see her best friend again. She puts Miss Pinky and Giggles back in the box and continues her search. The next box is full of some of her old school work so she knows the hatbox can't be far. She lifts up a large trash bag full of some of her old clothes and underneath it she finds the pink hatbox. She carries it upstairs to her room along with Chico.

When Fancy is finally alone in her room she opens the hatbox. It is full of photographs from her youth. She comes across a photo of her sitting on Santa's lap at age six, and then she finds her 7th grade class picture. The first thing she notices isn't how nerdy she looks in her turtleneck and corduroys, but how unhappy she looks. She's the only person not smiling amidst all the happy faces.

Finally she finds some photos from high school. There are many pictures of her and Shawn together – at lunch in the school cafeteria, hanging out at the mall, having a snowball fight during a blizzard, posing together at their senior prom and holding up their diplomas after graduation. There is a photo of Shawn posing in front of the Shawn-mobile when she first bought it. And there is a shot of Fancy laughing hysterically, trying unsuccessfully to hide her face from the camera. Fancy remembers that day vividly and recalls taking the photo:

Somehow she had gotten the idea in her head that it would be cute to shave off her eyebrows and draw them on instead. She had completely shaved off both of her already attractive and naturally arched brows, and used a black eye pencil to draw two thin, dramatic arcs in place of them. When she was finished, she looked in the mirror for a moment before deciding that while her new brows weren't exactly natural looking, they weren't all that bad either. It wasn't until she saw Shawn that she realized they looked completely ridiculous. Shawn cracked jokes about Fancy's penciled-on eyebrows all that day, even as she tried to snap a picture of them, despite Fancy's protests.

"Why the hell, ya eyebrows all the way up on ya forehead?" Shawn had asked. "It looks like somebody just scared the shit out of you! What the hell did you use? A Sharpie? I sure hope that shit ain't permanent, 'cause I can't be walkin' around with yo' ass if you gonna be lookin' like Latoya Jackson and shit."

Shawn always kept Fancy laughing. Fancy notices that she is smiling in every one of the photos in which she is with Shawn. It was hard for her not to be happy when she was around Shawn.

As she is placing the photos back in the box, Fancy sees something shiny on the bottom of it. It is the heart locket Shawn had given her ten years ago. She had forgotten all about it. The chain had broken a long time ago and she put it in the box, planning to have it repaired, but never having done so.

She picks the locket up and opens it. *Fancy. Maribel.* She reads both names as she runs her fingers over the embossed letters. Shawn had the locket engraved that way as a reminder to her not to forget who she is. Fancy remembers Shawn's words: *"Because even though you're my Fancy, I want you to remember to always stay true to Maribel – stay true to yourself, because no matter what you're wearing or what you got, you're still a beautiful person, inside and out."*

Fancy begins to cry as she hangs her head in shame. She realizes she has completely failed Shawn. With her elaborate lies and the great lengths to which she goes to maintain the façade of Fancy, she has not stayed true to anyone, especially not herself. Throughout the years she has changed so much that Maribel has gotten completely lost; only Fancy remains. But as she sits there crying in the dim light of her small lamp, the thing Fancy resents most about herself is the irreversible damage she unknowingly caused the previous night. She had selfishly insulted and distanced Shawn, and she feels that in doing so, *she* had killed her best friend. No, she wasn't drunk behind the wheel of the truck that struck Shawn's car, but had she kept her inconsiderate comments to herself, she and Shawn would have gone to Velvet as planned, and Shawn would have been with her instead of driving home in a rage.

"Shawn was right," she sobs to herself, remembering the last thing Shawn had said to her the previous night in the car; it was something about realizing who really cares about her before it's too late. The ironic finality of Shawn's last words to her torments Fancy into the early morning hours, until she feels she has not a tear left to cry. She finally falls asleep at 4:18 on her cold, tear-drenched pillow, with Chico in her arms.

Chapter 20

Fancy wakes up shortly after 11:00 the next morning. Her eyes are red, sore and swollen, and her head is throbbing. She gets out of bed and goes downstairs to get something to eat. As she is walking down the stairs she can see Rafael on the couch out of the corner of her eye.

"Good mor—"

Fancy is taken by surprise when she looks up to see Rafael sitting on the couch in his underwear eating a bowl of cereal.

"Ummmm, can you put some clothes on?" she asks, perturbed, looking away from him.

"Come on, you're a big girl," he replies with a smirk. "Don't act like you've never seen a man in his calzoncillos before."

Rather than argue with him, Fancy decides she will take it up with her mother later. Shaking her head, she continues into the kitchen.

After her scrambled eggs, raisin bagel and coffee, Fancy gets showered and dressed and heads over to Ms. Mercer's with the photos of Shawn.

Ms. Mercer opens the door and her puffy, bloodshot eyes tell Fancy that she, too, had been up late crying the previous night.

"Hi, Ms. Mercer."

"Come on in, Fancy."

"How you holding up?"

"As best I can."

"I hear you. Well, I found a bunch of pictures," Fancy says, handing Ms. Mercer two sets of photos. "These are ones just of Shawn, and those are pics of her with friends at school and stuff."

"Oh, thank you so much," Ms. Mercer says, excitedly looking through the photos. "These are great."

She finds to a photo of Shawn in a blonde afro wig that makes her chuckle.

"I remember that silly ass wig."

"That wig was hilarious," Fancy laughs in agreement.

"Awww, graduation. I was so proud of my baby. And here she go with her damn middle fingers up...I don't think we'll use that one."

They both laugh. The pictures provide joyful and funny memories for Ms. Mercer, and Fancy is glad she is able to help her find a moment of happiness in the midst of her sorrow. Before Fancy leaves, Ms. Mercer tells her Shawn's funeral is scheduled for Wednesday morning. This means she must finish her speech by tomorrow night.

During her walk home Fancy begins to brainstorm about what she will write in Shawn's eulogy. She's never written one before and has no idea where to start. She wonders if she should begin with a funny story about Shawn. *No, that wouldn't be appropriate*, she thinks to herself. *After all, it is a funeral*. Fancy wants to honor Shawn to the fullest extent, and comes to the conclusion that the best way to do so is by painting an accurate portrait of who Shawn was. *Yes*, she thinks, *that's the way Shawn would have wanted it.*

Throughout the day Fancy continues contemplating what to write. She ends up putting it off until the day before the funeral. That night she irons her black belted wrap dress and hangs it on her closet door. Then finally she lies across her bed with her pen and notebook. She takes a deep breath and, feeling the pressure of the impending deadline, she simply writes whatever comes to mind. This leads to a lot of scribbling out as words, sentences and even entire paragraphs get the chop. Fancy fills her wastebasket to the brim with tear-soaked tissues and crumpled pages of text that *just isn't good enough*. Four-and-a-half hours later, she tears one final page out of her notebook – her finished speech. She is happy with what she has written. She only hopes she can manage to get through it without breaking down in tears. She folds the sheet of paper into a neat square and puts it on her nightstand before turning off the lamp and drifting off to sleep.

Chapter 21

Fancy is nervous as she walks into the church the following morning. She knows seeing Shawn's body is going to be difficult, and as this is her final goodbye, she hopes the eulogy she's prepared is adequate. Standing in the foyer, she peers through the open doors into the chapel. Before entering, she stops to admire three large boards displaying various photos of Shawn. She is unable to fight back her tears as she realizes how much she already misses her friend. She walks through the sanctuary doors and slowly starts down the aisle past rows of fellow mourners dressed in black. As she walks, she peers down the aisle at the large bouquets of colorful flowers surrounding the casket. She braces herself for the sight of Shawn's corpse, which is slowly revealed which each step she takes toward it. By the time she is in front of the casket, her vision is blurred by the tears rapidly flowing from her eyes. She knows this will be the last time she sees Shawn, but she also knows that in reality, what she's looking at is not Shawn. It is merely her body; the empty shell that once held the vibrant soul of her best friend, and now lies inside its final resting place: a cushy bed of cream velvet within a red oak coffin. Nevertheless she must bid her final farewells and hope that Shawn can hear them.

"Goodbye, Shawn," she whispers, planting a kiss on the corpse's cold cheek.

Fancy finds a seat and the service begins shortly after. There is a prayer, a scripture reading, the singing of a hymn and the recitation of a poem before Fancy is called to deliver the eulogy. Her heartbeat quickens when she hears her name, and she nervously walks up to the podium, clenching her speech in her clammy hands. She takes a deep breath before beginning.

"Good morning, everyone. When I sat down to write this eulogy I had no idea where to begin. I knew I wanted to talk about Shawn's legacy and what she is leaving us with, but it was hard to decide what to start with. I mean, Shawn had so many amazing qualities and there are just so many things I admired about her – her perseverance; her originality; her courage; her wisdom; her sense of humor; the way she cared for her friends and family. Shawn had a huge heart. There were so many times she allowed me to cry on her shoulder. She always listened to my problems and helped me overcome whatever I was going through. You could never stay sad or upset around Shawn for too long, because she was always there with a joke or a funny story to cheer you up. Shawn was also multi-talented. She was great at fixing cars, an excellent cook and amazing at math."

Several people in the audience look at each other in bewilderment.

Vanna B.

"Math?!" one of Shawn's younger cousin's blurts out, surprised. This exclamation prompts Fancy to divert from her planned speech.

"Yup, math! I remember once in 10th grade we had a substitute teacher in our math class. We had a big test the next day and the substitute was supposed to help us review for it, but she obviously knew nothing about algebra. She was fumbling and bumbling through the equations. We were all trying so hard not to laugh. But of course, Shawn couldn't hold her laugh back – or she just didn't want to. You should've seen the teacher's face when Shawn just burst out laughing. She was soooo mad! She said, 'Come here, young man.' So Shawn went up to the front of the classroom and the teacher said, 'Let's see if you can do a better job at teaching this class.' Shawn shrugged, took the chalk, went to the blackboard and actually started teaching the class! She breezed right through the review. And she really knew her stuff. I mean, she was able to break those equations down in a way that all of us understood so easily. It was amazing. Everyone was so surprised, but grateful too, because we all did well on the test."

Fancy looks out at the audience and every face is smiling back at her.

"That was Shawn, you know? She had so many hidden talents, and so many facets to her – you never knew what to expect. But I think the thing I admired most about Shawn was her individuality and the way she didn't care what anyone thought about her. Shawn's attitude was, '*This is me. Take it or leave it.*' And I loved that about her. She always tried to instill that in those around her. She urged us to see that when it comes to being yourself, those that mind don't matter, and those that matter don't mind. I truly hope I can become more like Shawn in that way."

For a moment Fancy's mind wanders back to the night of Shawn's death and Shawn's last words to her in the car. Fancy hangs her head and begins to cry. She wishes that Shawn hadn't been right. She wishes that it wasn't too late. She wishes she could rewind time and relive that night. She'd give anything for a second chance to go back and change the course of events that occurred that night. Fancy lifts her head and through her teary eyes she sees a room full of faces staring back at her. An usher hands her a tissue and she blots her eyes and tries to regroup herself before continuing.

"I'm sorry. I'm just still in shock. This whole thing is so surreal to me. It's gonna be so hard without her, but you know what? I am so glad and feel truly honored to have been lucky enough to have had such an amazing friend for so long. Even though she's no longer here with us physically, Shawn will remain in our hearts forever. Her memory will live on with us until we meet her again. Rest in peace, Shawn. We'll miss you."

After Shawn's memorial service, everyone proceeds to the cemetery for the burial and then finally to the church's dining room for the reception. By the end of the day Fancy is exhausted. She kicks off her shoes as soon as she walks in the house and goes upstairs to take a relaxing bath before bed.

She is both disappointed and disgusted to find the bathroom filthy. The sink is covered with beard shavings, the bath tub has a gray ring around it and the toilet has been left unflushed. If Fancy hadn't already suspected Rafael as the culprit, the raised toilet seat and dirty men's briefs on the floor would have been a dead giveaway.

Fancy storms down the hall to her mother's bedroom and pounds on the door.

"Mom!" she yells, interrupting the muffled laughter coming from behind it.

"What, Fancy?" Anna asks, holding her robe closed as she opens the door. "Why you banging on my door like you loca?"

"Tell your nasty ass boyfriend he needs to clean up after himself! He ain't the only one that uses the bathroom!"

"Cálmate, Fancy. I'll clean it in the morning."

"He's a grown man, Mom. He should clean up his own damn mess. I can't even come home and take a bath. He got a nasty ass ring around the tub, hair all in the sink, piss in the toilet—"

"Hey mamacita," Rafael yells from the bed, "if it's yellow, let it mellow!"

"What?"

"If it's brown flush it down!" Rafael erupts into a roaring laugh.

"You see that? He has no respect for you!"

"No, Fancy. *You* have no respect for me! You came banging on my door over this nonsense? Okay, sometimes the bathroom gets dirty. If it's dirty why don't you clean it? Especially since you live here for free! You don't pay any rent or bills and you come to me complaining about *my man*? When you get your own house and your own man then you can do what you want, okay?"

And with that Anna goes back into her room, slamming the door in Fancy's face.

After giving the bath tub a thorough scrubbing, Fancy enjoys a nice long soak. When she's finished, she slips into her pajamas, brushes her teeth and lies down in bed. Shortly after she dozes off she is awakened by loud screams and moans coming from her mother's room, accompanied by the steady banging of the headboard against the wall.

"Oh my God," Fancy groans to herself pulling the pillow over her head. "I gotta get the hell outta here."

Chapter 22

Fancy is irritable after the long, restless night. When she goes downstairs to the kitchen for breakfast, her mother is sitting at the table drinking a cup of coffee. Fancy walks past Anna silently. She takes a mug from the cupboard and slams the cabinet door closed before reaching into the utensil drawer. She grabs a teaspoon and forcefully pushes the drawer closed, causing the silverware inside to rattle loudly as it bangs shut.

"You got a problem?" Anna asks, sensing Fancy's attitude.

"Yeah, actually I do, Mom. I got a problem with being kept awake all night by the sound of you and that filthy scumbag fucking!"

"Who the hell do you think you are? Some princess that I gotta tiptoe around my own house for? I don't think so! And you better watch how you're talking to me!"

"I'm not asking you to tiptoe. All I'm asking for is some common courtesy! I'm pregnant, I'm stressed and you knew I had just come back from Shawn's funeral. All I wanted was some sleep, for Christ's sake! Bad enough I had to clean the damn bathroom after that nasty ass slob you got staying here."

"You know what, Fancy? You're nothing but an ungrateful little bitch! If I was living somewhere for free, where I paid no bills and didn't even buy food, I would keep my mouth closed and show some damn gratitude. But no, not Princess Fancy. Instead you're constantly complaining, always giving me attitude and now even disrespecting my man. You need to find someplace else to stay – and fast."

"Well, finally something we can agree on! Don't worry...I'll be out of here as soon as I can."

Fancy decides to go out for breakfast instead. Since she doesn't have any money, she reaches into her mother's purse and quickly snatches a five-dollar bill before grabbing her coat and heading out the door.

Walking along the littered sidewalk, Fancy wishes she could move out of her mother's house immediately and get her own place. She knows she will continue to be stressed if she stays at Anna's, and that it is unhealthy for her pregnancy. She also knows, however, that since she has nowhere else to go, she will just have to endure living there until an alternative arises. *I need a job*, Fancy thinks to herself, realizing that is the only way she will be able to come up with the money to move out and get her own place.

On her way to get breakfast, she purchases a copy of the Philadelphia Daily News from a man selling them on Roosevelt Boulevard. When she arrives at Dunkin Donuts, she orders a small coffee with extra cream and extra sugar and a glazed donut. She sits down by a window with her breakfast and opens the newspaper, flipping directly to the classifieds in the back. She looks at the rentals section to get an idea of how much a one-bedroom apartment would cost her monthly – around $650. Next she turns to the help wanted ads. She takes a black pen from her coat pocket as she begins to scan the job listings. One immediately catches her attention:

Administrative assistant for law firm: Duties include answering phones, bookkeeping, appointment setting and assisting associates.

Sounds good...I can do that, she thinks to herself as she circles the ad. Then she continues reading and sees that a college degree is required. She draws a big X through the ad and continues searching. The next listing she sees is for an aide at a daycare center:

Busy daycare center seeking aide to assist teachers with activities. Must be great with children and pass background check.

No problem, Fancy thinks. But she reads on only to find that the position requires a minimum of three years of experience working with children.

As she continues reading through the ads, it begins to seem that every job listed requires a degree or some type of related work experience, neither of which she has. Then she comes across the one ad that is the exception:

Star's Cabaret, Philadelphia's premier upscale gentlemen's club, is hiring beautiful cocktail waitresses. No experience required. Come in Mon. through Wed., noon to 3 PM for interview.

Now there's a job I can do! Remembering that it is Wednesday, Fancy quickly finishes her donut and hurries home to get ready to go to Star's. She showers, does her hair and make-up and dresses in a short black miniskirt, black knee boots and a pink V-neck sweater that shows plenty of cleavage.

Walking up to Star's, Fancy realizes that it really doesn't look all that upscale. With its neon sign and blinking lights it actually looks like a pretty cheesy place. Nevertheless, she has heard of it many times before and knows that it is one of Philly's most popular strip clubs. She walks in and approaches the bored-looking hostess sitting behind the front counter.

"Hi," Fancy says, "I'm here about the cocktail waitress position."

The girl looks her up and down.

"Okay, wait right here."

She disappears around a corner and is back in less than a minute.

"He'll be right out."

A couple minutes later a tall 40-something man with slicked back dirty blonde hair and a thin gold rope chain appears from around the corner. He too looks Fancy up and down before sticking out his hand for her to shake.

"Name's Lev," he says. "I'm the manager here."

Vanna B.

With his deep voice and thick accent, he sounds like a Russian gangster straight out of a movie.

"Hi, I'm Fancy. Nice to meet you."

"Fancy, huh? Come with me, Fancy."

Fancy follows him around the corner and into his office, where he gestures for her to have a seat.

"So you want to be a cocktail waitress?"

"I sure do."

"Well I'm not going to hire you as a cocktail waitress and I'll tell you why. You, my dear, should be dancing. You've got a beautiful face, gorgeous body and you'd make ten times more money, easy."

"Thank you but no, I don't think that's for me. I mean, the whole getting naked thing just—"

"Oh come on," he rudely interrupts. "It's just tits and ass. Nothing anybody hasn't seen before. You can turn on the TV and see that nowadays. Anyway we don't do full nudity...just G-strings. The only time you get naked is in the private rooms, and that's even more money."

"I just don't think I could do it."

"I bet you could after a few drinks. All the girls that say they can't do it loosen up after a couple drinks and then they love it. I'll tell you what – stick around for a little bit, have a few drinks on us, talk to some of the dancers and if you feel up to it you can get on stage and audition. Sound good?"

"Okay," Fancy says hesitantly. "But I seriously doubt it's gonna happen."

Lev leads Fancy out into the club's main room, which surprisingly looks a lot nicer than the outside suggests. It is a plush-looking place with large flat screen televisions, red carpeted floors, leather chairs and two stages with gold poles. The club is pretty empty. There is a handful of customers and only about six or seven dancers there. One girl is on stage lazily leaning her back against the pole as she slowly gyrates. Fancy can't help but wonder how the girl managed to get hired.

Lev sits Fancy down at the end of the bar and introduces her to a pretty purple-haired bartender with multiple facial piercings.

"Suzie, this is Fancy. Give her whatever she wants."

Then he turns to Fancy and squeezes her shoulder.

"Suzie will take good care of you, baby."

"So what'll it be?" Suzie asks.

Fancy remembers hearing that it is okay to drink wine while you are pregnant, so she asks Suzie for a glass of Merlot.

"Sure, hon."

Suzie pours the wine and sets the glass in front of Fancy before leaning in closer to talk to her.

"So you wanna dance here?"

"I don't know. I came in because I saw an ad in the paper for cocktail waitresses."

"Yeah, like 85% of the girls that come in for waitressing jobs end up dancing because they know they'll make way more money. You could totally do it though. Nothing to be scared about. These losers will worship you and give you all their money. It's really easy, especially after a few drinks. I think you'd do great. You're hot."

Suzie looks up and calls out to two dancers that are walking by.

"Trinity! Crystal!" she yells, motioning for them to come over. "Isn't she hot?"

"Ooooh, she is!" squeals the petite, tanned Asian one wearing a baby blue one-piece with white fishnet thigh-high stockings. "She's a dime."

"You gonna work here?" asks the thin redhead in the silver bikini.

"I don't know yet."

"Her name's Fancy," Suzie says.

"Already got your stage name picked out, huh?" says the Asian. "Well I'm Trinity and this is Crystal."

Since business in the club is slow, Trinity and Crystal sit down at the bar to talk and drink with Fancy. She asks them lots of questions as they continue to try to persuade her to join them at Star's. The girls seem to be happy working there. Fancy learns that Crystal has her own place, two nice cars and money saved in the bank.

Contemplating her decision, Fancy weighs the pros and cons in her head: *It's good money and it is pretty easy. Plus I should take advantage of my looks while I still have them – who knows what my body will look like after the baby! I don't really like the idea of dancing in my underwear, but where else can I make a bunch of money fast, without any type of degree or experience? I could just do it for a couple months so I can get an apartment and save up for the baby.*

An hour or so later, after lots of chitchat and several glasses of wine, Trinity and Crystal pull Fancy over to the stairs leading to the stage.

"Come on girl," Trinity says, "stop bullshittin' and get your ass up there."

"Yeah, take it off!" yells Crystal.

Suzie has retrieved Lev from his office.

"She's ready, Lev."

"Noooo, I'm not ready!" Fancy laughs.

"Come on, I got a hundred bucks for you if you do it right now," says Lev, waving a hundred-dollar bill.

"Hmmm, well that does kind of sweeten the deal," Fancy says, "but I don't like this song, though. Wait until a good song comes on."

"Stop making excuses," Crystal says. "The DJ can play whatever song you want."

"I don't even know what song I want. I'll just wait 'til he plays one I like."

"I got a song for you," says Trinity. "Be right back."

She dashes over to the DJ booth, says something to him quickly and then walks back over.

The DJ stops the song that is playing and puts on "Fancy" by Drake. Fancy smiles and shakes her head.

"I should have known."

Trinity, Crystal and Suzie start singing the lyrics along with the song as they push Fancy on stage.

"Go, go, go 'head! Go, go, go 'head! Oh you fancy, huh? Oh you fancy, huh?"

Fancy finally gives in and two-steps coyly but sexily onto the stage. When she reaches the pole she holds onto it while strutting around it then drops down to the floor, spreading her knees. This makes her skirt rise up, exposing her black thong. The girls and the few patrons clap, cheer and whistle loudly, boosting Fancy's confidence. Feeling bold, she moves her hips seductively as she takes off her sweater and swings it around rodeo style before throwing it across the club. She shimmies out of her skirt and flips her hair wildly. Before she knows it the song is over and her exotic dancing debut is met with a round of approving applause. She picks up her skirt before walking off stage. Suzie gives Fancy her sweater and Lev hands over the hundred-dollar bill.

"You got the job, baby."

Chapter 23

Fancy sits on an examination table in her neighborhood clinic waiting to be seen by the doctor. She is visiting for her first monthly prenatal check-up since she found out she was pregnant. Fancy has already had her weight and blood pressure taken by a nurse, but, once again, the clinic is crowded, which means the doctors are very busy. Fancy has been sitting on the examination table wearing a paper gown for nearly forty-five minutes. She stands up to stretch her stiff legs and the gown sticks to her buttocks. She looks at her clothes sitting on the chair and considers getting dressed and leaving. But before she can reach for them the door springs open. Dr. Patel, the same doctor Fancy had seen during her last visit to the clinic, picks up Fancy's chart on her way in and quickly looks it over.

"Hello again, Ms. Alvarez," she says. "Sorry about the wait. As you can see we are very busy."

"As usual," Fancy adds.

Dr. Patel washes her hands and puts on a pair of latex gloves before instructing Fancy to lie back and place her feet in the stirrups. She gently inserts two fingers to check Fancy's cervix. Then she removes the gloves, discarding them in a waste bin, and presses various spots on Fancy's abdomen.

Afterwards, she instructs Fancy to sit back up on the table.

"Let's take a listen to your baby's heart," Dr. Patel says. She uses a Doppler to amplify the baby's heartbeat. Fancy's face is illuminated with joy as she listens to the rhythmic beats of her unborn child's heart.

Wow, she thinks, *I'm really going to be a mother! There is life growing inside me. What a gift! I can't wait to meet my baby!*

Fancy's pregnancy is finally starting to seem real to her, and she is beginning to get excited about it. For the first time ever, instead of being fearful, she is actually looking forward to motherhood.

"That's my little angel in there," she says, grinning from ear to ear.

"Yep," says Dr. Patel, "and he or she has a very strong, healthy sounding heartbeat. You both seem to be doing just fine."

"Well that's great news."

"In another few weeks you'll be able to find out the sex of the baby."

"I'm actually not planning on finding out. I want to wait and be surprised."

"Oh, that'll be fun. Now Maribel, it says in your chart that you are currently unemployed. Do you have somewhere to stay with heat and hot water?"

"Yes."

"Do you have access to enough food?"

"Yes."

"Do you or does anyone in your home smoke cigarettes?"

"No."

"Do you use illegal and/or street drugs?"

"No."

"Do you drink alcohol?"

"Well, I did drink a little the other day, but it was just wine, though. Wine's okay, right?"

"How much wine did you drink?"

"Um, I guess like three or four glasses."

Dr. Patel peers at Fancy over the top of her glasses.

"Three or four glasses is way too much alcohol. Drinking like that could severely harm your unborn baby."

"Really? But I heard that it was okay to drink wine while you're pregnant."

"There are some schools of thought that a glass of wine – *one* glass – every once in a while will not do damage. But many medical professionals, myself included, believe that no amount of alcohol is acceptable for a pregnant woman to consume."

"Wow, I had no idea. I'm glad you told me."

Dr. Patel hands Fancy a folder.

"Here's some information about what foods you should eat and how to take care of yourself while you are pregnant. Make sure you get yourself some prenatal vitamins – any brand will do."

"Okay."

Vanna B.

"And no alcohol!" Dr. Patel says, shaking her finger at Fancy, as if reprimanding a child.
"Okay, geez, I got it. No drinking."

Chapter 24

Fancy walks into Star's with her Louie duffle bag over her shoulder and her stomach in knots. It is her first day of work as an exotic dancer and she is a bundle of nerves. On her way up to the dressing room, she peeps into the club's main room. It is Saturday, one of the busiest nights, and unlike the day she auditioned, there is a thick crowd. She is extremely anxious about having to perform without being able to relieve her insecurities with alcohol. She walks back into the hallway and continues toward the dressing room.

With a sweaty palm she turns the knob to the dressing room door and pushes it open. As she enters she is greeted by the bright lighting and the buzz of chattering women. All the ladies in the room turn to see who is entering. After a quick look they continue conversing, getting dressed, applying their make-up and styling their hair. Only one woman's attention remains fixed on Fancy. Sensing she is being watched, Fancy turns to see a beautiful Latina eyeballing her. Her build is similar to Fancy's and she, too, has long dark hair. Unlike Fancy, though, the girl has numerous tattoos scattered all over her body: a lion on her right forearm, "Julio" on the side of her neck, a golden crown over her left breast, a gun on her right hip and the flag of Puerto Rico on the other. Most people quickly look away when caught staring at someone, but not her. Feeling somewhat awkward, Fancy flashes a friendly smile which, surprisingly, goes unreturned. The woman maintains her cold stare. Fancy is unsure of what to make of it, but certainly finds it a little weird. She can feel the woman's eyes following her as she makes her way across the room; she can feel her studying her anatomy and analyzing her every movement.

"Fancyyy!" She turns to see a topless Trinity walking toward her. "Hey sexy!"

She gives Fancy a tight hug, pressing her bare breasts against Fancy's clothed ones.

"Hey, Trinity. How are you?"

"I'm good, mami. You ready to get this money?"

"I'm here." Fancy sighs, shrugging.

"I know you're not trippin', girl. Just have a couple drinks and do what you did the other day. Come on, you gotta meet Lana. She's the house mom."

"House mom?"

"Yeah, she just pretty much makes sure we're all doing what we're supposed to be doing: dressing right, getting to the stage on time – shit like that. You'll love her. She's super sweet and she's been working here since, like, the beginning of time. She used to dance here, back when they first opened."

Trinity leads Fancy past the mirrors and lockers to a small office in the back of the dressing area. She knocks on the open door and Lana, who is at her desk on a phone call, motions for them to come in and sit down. Lana puts her cigarette out in the ashtray and raises a finger to let them know she'll be with them in a minute.

Lana is a bony, middle-aged woman. She has big platinum blonde hair, a dark, unnatural-looking tan and deep wrinkles, which Fancy deduces are from a combination of frequent tanning and years of cigarette smoking. On the wall behind her is a poster of her in her younger years. She is posing naked on a bearskin rug and the poster reads, *Lana Villari: Live at Star's Cabaret*. Lana finishes up her conversation and hangs up the phone.

"Sorry about that, girls. Who's this baby doll, Trinity?"

"This is Fancy. Today's her first day."

"Oh! Welcome, sweetie! I'm Lana. I'm here to help you with whatever you need, so don't be afraid to ask. Have you ever danced before?"

"No, I'm new to the...profession."

"Well we've got a lot of things to go over. But don't worry, we'll get you all nice and comfy and ready."

Trinity goes to finish getting dressed while Lana goes over a plethora of information including Star's fees, scheduling policies, dancers' code of conduct and wardrobe requirements. Afterwards she asks Fancy if she has any questions. She just has one.

"So, in the private rooms," Fancy begins, "it's just dancing right? I mean, the guys won't try to do anything else, will they?"

"Oh sweetie, you'll have guys asking you to do all types of things. But just let 'em know this ain't that kind of establishment. You can touch them if you want, but they can't touch you. Anybody gives you a hard time, security's right outside the door. Just let 'em know and they'll get rid of the guy, quick."

Lana sets Fancy up with a locker and shows her where extra make-up and feminine hygiene supplies are kept in case she should need them.

"Well, you better go ahead and get dressed, hon. You're on the main stage in 20 minutes."

Fancy looks into her bag at what she brought to wear. Since she hadn't had any money to buy anything new, she brought a couple bikini swimsuits and some lingerie sets that she already owned. She decides to put on a black and red lace bra and boy short set with a black thong underneath. She did her make-up before she left home so she just has to touch it up. Fancy changes her lip color from a shiny pink gloss to a more dramatic red matte lipstick, and brushes her long, thick mane. With her rosy cheeks, she somewhat resembles a doll, and her smoky black eye shadow gives her eyes a cat-like appearance. She looks at her scantily clad reflection in the mirror while trying to muster up some courage. *I can do this! I **have** to do this!*

For the money; for the baby; for myself. I know I can do it. I did it before and I can do it again!

Her reflection is joined in the mirror by Trinity's. "Brought you something," she says, handing Fancy a glass of wine. "This'll help you loosen up."

Fancy slowly takes the glass, staring at it as if it were an alien object from another planet.

"You okay?" Trinity asks.

"Yeah...but um, I don't need the drink," she says, pushing the glass back into Trinity's hand.

"You sure? You said you were a little nervous."

"Yeah, it's cool. I'm trying to cut back."

"Alright then," Trinity says before taking a big sip. "Suit yourself."

"Hey, who's that girl over there?" Fancy asks, glancing at the woman who had been staring at her.

"In the black? Oh, that's Bella. She's Puerto Rican like you. Actually you guys kind of look alike."

"Oh so all Ricans look alike, huh?" Fancy jokes.

"Yea, y'all are just like us Asians," Trinity playfully jokes back.

The two of them laugh.

"Well, you do kinda look like her over there," Fancy says, pointing to another Asian dancer in the room.

"Hell no!" Trinity snaps back. "She's Korean and I'm Cambodian. Not even close! You and Bella, though. Y'all could be sisters."

"The only reason I asked about her is 'cause she was staring at me when I walked in – like *hard*."

"Hey, who knows? Maybe she likes you."

"Nah, she wasn't lookin' at me like she liked me. She looked like she had an attitude."

"I don't know then. I've only been here for a little over a week so I don't know everybody like that yet. Maybe she's jealous."

Their conversation is interrupted by Lana calling out Fancy's name. She is standing at the dressing room door, waving her over. "Come on, sweetie. It's show time."

Fancy's heart begins pounding so hard she is sure everyone can see it beating through her chest. With desperation in her eyes, she turns to Trinity hoping for some epic advice that will erase her fears, but all she says is, "Go, get 'em, girl!"

Fancy walks over to Lana, inhaling and exhaling deeply in an attempt to calm her nerves. They enter the club's main room and are greeted by loud music booming over the buzz of conversation, and a hazy mixture of cigarette and cigar smoke. The club is packed and she can feel herself shaking as Lana guides her toward the stairs leading to the stage.

"Lana, I'm really scared," Fancy finally confesses.

"Oh come on, sweetie. It's too late to back out now."

"I'm not. It's just...well, what if I'm not any good? I can't do any pole tricks. And at my audition I was drunk, so it was easy. But now—"

"Look at that girl on stage," Lana interrupts.

Fancy turns her attention to the waif thin brunette shimmying beside the pole.

"Do you think she can dance?" asks Lana sarcastically.

"Not really," Fancy giggles.

"Hell no, the girl can't dance! But she's pretty and she smiles and she looks like she's having a great time. And ya know what? She's one of our top earners."

"Really?"

"Yep. The stage is just something you have to do – a small part of the job. But the majority of your money will be made giving private dances. When you get off stage and make your rounds, that's the part that really counts. Be nice, smile, listen to their bullshit stories and persuade 'em to get a private dance."

"Okay."

"When I first started dancing I hated getting on stage too. The crowd made me nervous as hell. You know what helped me? I'd find one guy in the club and focus on him. I'd act like he was the only person in the audience and that made it a lot less intimidating. You see that fat guy sitting in the middle there? Focus on him and his gut."

Fancy chuckled.

"Don't look around at all the other eyes watching. Just look at him."

"Okay, I'll try it."

The song that is playing ends, and the skinny brunette slinks off the stage. Fancy realizes she forgot to give the DJ a list of songs she likes. She wonders what song he will play. Her question is answered when "Fancy," the same song she auditioned to, begins to play. Lana stretches her arm out toward the stairs, and Fancy begins walking up.

"And now," the DJ says over the music, "Star's Cabaret would like to introduce the newest addition to our amazing lineup. Please give a warm welcome to the beautiful, the talented, the luscious, lusty, Latina lover, FANCYYYYY!"

Fancy nervously switches onto the stage greeted by the crowd's applause. She can feel every pair of eyes in the building examining her body. She begins to dance to the music, looking up and sometimes down – anywhere that enables her to avoid looking at the faces of her audience. Her gaze eventually finds its way to Lana. Then Fancy remembers what Lana had said. She glances at the center table closest to the stage. The large, round man is sipping his beer and peering back at her. She locks her gaze on him and begins removing her bra. The man fidgets nervously. *Wow, he's more nervous than I am.* Fancy smiles at him and he sheepishly smiles back. She gets down on her hands and knees and crawls across the stage toward his table. She points at him and summons him with a curl of her finger. He looks around coyly before slowly rising and approaching the stage, dollars in hand. Fancy stands and removes her boy shorts, bending over right in front of him. He inserts each of the bills into the waistband of her thong, giving her a skirt of dollar bills. The song ends and Fancy collects her clothing and several bills from the stage floor. Once she is off stage she exhales a huge sigh of relief. Lana comes over and rubs her on her back.

"Good job, sweetie! You did great."

According to Lana and the other dancers, the hard part is over. The rest, they say, will be easy. Fancy begins walking around the room, approaching patrons to see if they would like a dance. The first few men decline, but give her small tips anyway. Then finally she meets a married couple who buys a table dance. She feels awkward and uncomfortable grinding on the strangers' laps. To make the time go faster she distracts herself with thoughts of the brighter future ahead of her – the future that will only be possible because of the money she's earning. She thinks of her baby and how great it will be when they're all settled in their own apartment – just the two of them.

Before she knows it the song is over. She collects her money and goes on to the next table – the fat man's table. He wants a private dance so they go into a private room. He seems very shy while they are talking and Fancy expects that he will be a gentleman during the dance. To her

Vanna B.

surprise she finds the man to have an entirely different disposition once they are alone. He is rude and crass. Despite her requests for him to stop, he repeatedly grabs her breasts and rubs his hands between her legs. Finally she calls for a bouncer who quickly escorts the disrespectful man out of the club.

Chapter 25

While Fancy likes the fast money she is making, she quickly realizes that stripping certainly has its downside. But the worst part about the job isn't getting naked for strangers, or even the stage performance. The worst part of being an exotic dancer – the part Fancy hates – is dealing with disrespectful patrons such as the fat man. She encounters countless customers who simply refuse to respect her limits. After almost two weeks she still hasn't gotten used to it. But she endures it. Night after night she goes to work at Star's. Some nights come and go without any incidents. Others are not so smooth.

One such night Fancy is in a private room with a customer, a short, stocky man with a thick mustache. Even though the lighting in the club is dim, the man keeps his dark sunglasses on. Fancy has been with him for almost a half-hour and finds it extremely weird and annoying that while she's dancing, he moans as if he's having sex. *Well, it could be worse*, Fancy thinks to herself as she dances on the man's lap. *At least he knows how to keep his hands to himself.* Suddenly Fancy is startled by the feeling of warm liquid on her thigh. She is horrified and disgusted when she realizes the fluid running down her leg is the man's semen.

"You asshole!" she yells, running out of the room. "That's fuckin' disgusting!" On her way to the bathroom, she tells the bouncers to get rid of the man and collect her $300 from him. Lana comes into the bathroom after her.

"Fancy, what happened, sweetie? You okay?"

"Yeah, I'm okay. That loser came on my leg...nasty fucker."

"Oh no, really? Okay, well take a breather and relax for a sec. After your get cleaned up why don't you head on up to VIP for a little bit?"

"Okay."

A few minutes later Fancy walks into the club's dimly lit VIP section and no sooner than she enters does she hear a familiar voice calling her name.

"Fuuuck," She whispers to herself, closing her eyes tightly.

Fancy immediately recognizes the voice as Jaslyn's. She turns to see Jaslyn is not alone. She is sitting at a table, drinking champagne with the last person on Earth she wants to see – Aaron. Fancy wishes she could disappear.

"Fancy?" says Jaslyn, "You strippin' now?"

"Wooow!" Aaron says loudly and dramatically.

"Well," Fancy explains, "I just started. And it's only temporary."

"Sure it is, girl," Jaslyn chuckles, flagging her, "That's what they all say."

"Oh wait, let me guess," says Aaron, "You need money for your baby, right?" Because you're pregnant...by me!"

He and Jaslyn erupt in laughter.

Fancy tries to remain calm and hide her anger.

"Why would I lie about being pregnant?"

"Oh I don't know," Aaron replies, "Maybe because you're a money-hungry ho. But then again, most strippers are."

He begins to laugh again and Jaslyn joins in.

Their taunting is really starting to get to Fancy now. She is beyond agitated but still maintains her composure. She speaks sternly, but does not raise her voice.

"You ain't shit, Aaron," Fancy says, shaking her head in disbelief. "I never met someone so two-faced in my whole life."

She then turns to Jaslyn with a look of utter disgust.

"And you...I knew you were a shady bitch, but I would have never expected you to just sit up in my face and laugh at me like we weren't hangin' out every fuckin' weekend. You're really showin' off for this clown."

"Bitch, you the only clown I see!" Jaslyn retorts, rolling her neck. "You're the one shakin' ya naked ass for money. You need a couple dollars, sweetie? I got you."

Jaslyn takes several dollar bills from her purse and throws them at Fancy.

Vanna B.

"Go ahead, you know you wanna pick 'em up."

At this point Fancy's blood is boiling. She looks at the champagne bottle on the table and envisions it shattering against Jaslyn's head. Then she imagines the thick plastic sole of her seven-inch platform shoe meeting Aaron's face as he rushes to help his bleeding date off the floor. But Fancy knows pulling a stunt like that will get her fired for sure. She simply smiles and walks away. A single tear rolls down her cheek. She quickly wipes it away before anyone notices.

Chapter 26

Fancy walks into the rental office of a quaint-looking apartment complex in Northeast Philadelphia. She had noticed the complex several times while riding past it during the bus ride to Brittany's house. She always thought it looked like a nice place to live, with its well-kept courtyard in which beautiful tulips and dogwood trees blossomed in the spring. She has an appointment to view a one-bedroom apartment and plans to find out the monthly rent and how much she'll need to move in.

The agent greets her when she walks in, and then grabs a set of keys from a hook behind his desk. As they walk to the second floor unit, he tells her all about the apartment complex and its features. Fancy can't wait to see it. When they arrive, he unlocks the door and ushers her in. While the apartment isn't quite as nice as the exterior suggests, it is, nonetheless, a suitable living space. It doesn't appear run-down, but it's nothing spectacular either – just an average apartment. It is a good size, though, and has fresh paint and new carpets. Fancy pictures herself sitting in the living room rocking her baby in her arms. She imagines pushing the baby's stroller around the sunny courtyard and relaxing under the shade of the flowering trees. She thinks the two of them would be comfortable there.

"So how much is the rent?"

"The rent is $700 a month and all utilities are included. We require first and last months' rent, as well as a $700 security deposit to move in."

"So I'd need a total of $2,100 to move in. Do you run credit checks?"

"While a credit check is not necessary, we do require proof of employment and two references. People like landlords or employers – current or previous – will do."

Fancy is relieved. She knows she would not pass a credit check. She could, however, use Lev and Lana as references.

Fancy spends the remainder of the afternoon visiting various stores and pricing furniture, household items and things for the baby. She decides the bedroom furniture and TV are the only essential items that must be purchased before she moves in. Everything else, she can get afterwards; and since the baby isn't due until July, she'll have plenty of time to prepare for his or her arrival. Fancy sees a beautiful cherry wood bedroom set and a nice 46-inch flat screen television she'd like for her apartment. These items add an additional $2,500 to her move-in costs, so adding in a little extra for smaller necessities, she figures she'll need about $5,000 to move into her apartment.

That night after work Fancy counts $650 in tips. Unfortunately, half of it has to be turned in to

Lana to cover Star's fees. Still, she remains optimistic. *I'll have my apartment soon*, she thinks to herself, as she begins to count out the club's half. Trinity enters the dressing room and kicks off her platform heels.

"Girrrl, I am so glad I'm off tomorrow," she says, rubbing her tired feet.

"You ain't the only one."

"We should hit the mall."

"Cool. Let's do it."

"Where do you live? I'll pick you up."

"Nah, it's okay. I'll just meet you there."

"But you don't drive, do you? I know you catch cabs to work. You gonna catch a cab all the way to King of Prussia? Just tell me where you live and I'll come grab you."

Fancy knows Trinity is right. It is a very long ride to the mall.

"Okay," she says hesitantly, "but...I live in the hood though – Olney."

"Girl, please...I'm from South Philly. Olney is like the burbs compared to my hood."

"Alright then," Fancy laughs "What time you wanna go?"

"I don't know. I'll call you in the morning."

"Don't call too early. I'm gonna stay here 'til they lock up and practice on the pole."

"Awww shit. Tryna step your game up, huh?"

"Yup."

"That's whassup. Aight girl, talk to you tomorrow."

"Get home safe, Trin."

Fancy goes back into the main room, which is now empty aside from a few bartenders and several other miscellaneous staff members who are cleaning up. A complete stranger to the pole, Fancy is unsure where to begin. She tries to climb the pole but fails miserably. Her weak, untrained legs are unable to hold her weight and she quickly realizes she needs to start with something a little easier. *Damn, that shit is harder than it looks*, she thinks to herself, rubbing her sore calf muscles. She tries to imitate a simple spin she's seen some of the other girls do. She wraps her right leg around the pole and pushes off with the left, holding on with just one hand. For a second, she is spinning, but she loses her grip and falls to the stage floor. She is startled by the sound of laughter and looks up to see Bella and several of the other girls who have stopped to watch her on their way out. Bella, walks toward her clapping her hands.

"Wow!" she says sarcastically, "That was...entertaining."

The girls behind her continue laughing.

"You should really leave that to the pros, 'cause pole work is obviously not your thing."

"Yeah, I know I can use some work," Fancy laughs, dusting herself off. "That's why I'm staying late to practice."

Even though Bella is being rude, Fancy is hoping to win her over with kindness. She is new and doesn't want to make enemies.

"Maybe you can help me out sometime…teach me a few tricks."

Bella rolls her eyes.

"Sorry, sweetie. Bella don't do charity. Be careful on that thing, though. You wouldn't wanna hurt that pretty little face."

Bella and the girls leave and shortly after, Fancy does too.

Vanna B.

Chapter 27

Fancy thought she had an addiction to designer labels, but the following day at the mall, she learns that hers is nothing compared to Trinity's. Trinity only shops in high-end stores, and if she sees something she wants, she buys it, regardless of the price. Fancy wonders how much money Trinity has saved up working as an exotic dancer and how long it will take her to save up enough to move.

"How fast do you think I can make $5,000, Trin?"

"Girl, you can do that in a week."

"Yeah right."

"You can...if you really want it. Just remember a closed mouth don't get fed, and closed legs don't get bread."

Fancy looks at Trinity with a blank stare.

"Don't act like you don't know what I'm talkin' about, Fancy. You've never done nothin' strange for some change?"

Trinity laughs but Fancy knows she isn't joking.

"You mean—"

"Yeah, datin'. I'm sure you get offers all the time for sex and blowjobs."

"I thought that wasn't allowed."

"Technically it's not, but all the girls do it."

"Really? All of them?"

"Yup. Some of the newbies – like yourself – think they're too good to date, but when offered the right amount, anybody'll give in."

"Not me," Fancy says, shaking her head. "It would make me feel dirty, like I was a whore – no offense."

"None taken. Ain't no shame in my game. I see it like this: it's no different than a one-night stand. I know you've had at least one before."

"Well, yeah, but it was a mistake. I was drunk. That was different."

"The only difference is you gave it up for free! You may talk that goody two-shoes shit now, but when you start comparing how much you're making to how much the rest of us are making, you'll start to change your tune."

"How old are you anyway, Trin?"

"Eighteen."

"Are you serious?"

"Yup. I'll be 19 in May."

"Damn, I knew you were young but—"

"How old are you?"

"I'm 27."

"That's cool. You can be my big sis."

"Why are you dancing? You're so young. You still have your whole life ahead of you. There's still time for you to go to school and to do better things with your life."

"I hate school. I didn't even finish high school. I ran away from home in 11th grade."

Vanna B.

"So you've been on your own ever since?"

"Yup. It's just me and my boyfriend now. I met Vin a few months ago and moved in with him a couple weeks ago."

"And he doesn't mind you dancing?"

"Nope, as long as I'm making money."

"He knows about the dating and stuff?"

"Hell no, girl! He'd kick my ass!"

Fancy and Trinity go to Neiman Marcus where they try on tons of shoes. Trinity is buying four pairs. Fancy really likes a pair she's tried on, but she knows she has to save up so she can move.

"You have *got* to get those," Trinty insists. "They're hot!"

"Nah, I'm trying to save up so I can get an apartment. These are $350."

"Girl, you can make that back in half a night. Stop playing. You gotta enjoy your money, otherwise there's no point in working."

Trinity *does* have a point. And the shoes *are* awesome. Fancy decides she will buy the shoes – but nothing else.

"Oh my God...that bag!" Trinity says, nearly drooling over a handbag in the Gucci store. "That shit is super cute, right?"

"Yeah, it is," Fancy replies dreamily, although she is actually looking past the handbag, eyeing a brown and tan monogram diaper bag, thinking she *must* have it.

Trinity notices her ogling the bag.

"Um, you do know that's a diaper bag, right? For baby crap."

"Yeah, I know."

"You got a bun in the oven?"

Fancy smiles a big, proud smile.

"Awww, congratulations mama! That's so sweet. You must only be a couple of months – you're not showing at all yet."

"Yeah, I'm not due until July 17th."

The bag costs Fancy $900 and she swears to herself it is the last thing she is buying...until she sees the matching hat, booties and blanket, which add up to an additional $500. Before she knows it, Fancy has spent nearly all she has earned since she started working at Star's. She leaves the mall broke and feeling disappointed in herself.

Her mother is in the living room when she walks in the house. Fancy knows she won't make it upstairs without a few snide remarks from her.

"Neiman Marcus, huh?" says Anna, eyeing the shopping bags, "and Gucci!"

"Don't start, Mom."

"Looks like you're really saving up to move," she says sarcastically.

"It's just a few things for the baby, Mom."

"Oh yeah, because Gucci for the baby is so much more important than a place to live. You're losing sight of your priorities already! What happened to saving for an apartment and quitting the club? I guess you plan on being a stripper for the rest of your life."

"Mind your business!" Fancy shouts. "I'm grown! I can do what I want!"

"It *is* my business! You may be grown but you're still under my roof and you're still depending on me. And from the looks of things, I'll be supporting your child too."

Deciding to diffuse the situation before the argument escalates further, Fancy takes a deep breath and regains her composure.

"I didn't spend that much, Mom," she says calmly. "I'm still saving. I'll have the money soon."

And with that she walks up the stairs and into her room.

Fancy knows that her mother is right this time. *Damn*, Fancy thinks to herself, looking at the receipts from her mall trip. *I really shouldn't have spent all this money. I was on my way to getting my apartment, now I'm back at square one.*

She realizes there is no point in beating herself up over it and vows to stay on track from now on – no more frivolous spending. *Well, at least most of it was for the baby*, she rationalizes with herself. She holds up the Gucci booties and hat, admiring them. *My baby is gonna be flyyyy!*

Chapter 28

Fancy is at work on a Wednesday afternoon and business is slower than usual. After her turn on stage, she circles the room in boredom. All of the patrons are busy with other girls. She sees a group of three fifty-something African-American men at a table near the bar. Two of them are getting lap dances. The third is quietly sipping his beer, staring off into space. A curvy blonde dancer plops down on his lap, startling him. The man looks more annoyed than interested, and after a brief exchange of words the blonde gets up and leaves, empty-handed. Fancy thinks the man would appreciate a more subtle approach – one like hers. She walks over and sits in the empty seat next to him.

"Hi," she says. "How are you?"

"Not too bad. And yourself?"

"I'm good. My name's Fancy."

She extends her hand and the man reaches out and shakes it firmly.

"Pleasure to meet you, Fancy. I'm Lou."

"Nice to meet you, too. I couldn't help but notice you look a little bored."

"Is it that obvious?" Lou asks, with a half-smile. "Yeah, these guys dragged me in here. It's not exactly my scene – no offense to you, of course."

"No, I understand. There are a million other places I'd rather be right now, too."

"You do seem a little out of place here."

Fancy stares at Lou awaiting an explanation.

"You seem like a classy girl. What are you doing working in a joint like this?"

"I need the money. I don't exactly have a lot of options when it comes to work."

Lou's friends are finished getting their lap dances and are preparing to leave. Lou reaches into the pocket of his khakis and pulls out his wallet. Instead of a tip, though, he gives Fancy his business card.

"If you ever get sick of this place and want another job, you can come work at one of my grocery stores. It doesn't pay a whole lot, but it does come with medical and dental benefits."

"Okay," Fancy says, reaching out and taking the business card. "Thanks."

Lou takes a final sip of his beer and gets up to leave. "Good talking to you, Fancy."

"Bye."

After Lou has gone, Fancy looks at the card. *Val-U Rite Markets*. Fancy is familiar with the small, local chain of discount grocery stores. *Yeah right*, she thinks to herself. *He must be crazy*. She goes into the dressing room to check her make-up and sees Trinity rummaging through her locker.

"Hey, Trin."

"Hey, Fancy. Rough night for tips, huh?"

"Yeah, it's dead out there tonight."

"I'm working a private party Friday night. You can join me if you're interested."

"A private party? I don't know."

"It's just a few guys from my neighborhood. They're cool."

"Well, maybe. Just dancing though, right?"

"Yeah, girl. Just dancing."

"Okay then."

"Cool. I'll pick you up at eleven."

Suddenly, Bella storms over and roughly snatches Trinity by the arm, pulling her to the side and bumping Fancy in the process.

Ok, this shit is getting out of hand, Fancy thinks to herself, *now she's invading my space*. Fancy isn't going to ignore her blatant rudeness this time.

"Excuse you," Fancy says, annoyed. "You just bumped me."

"Oh really?" Bella asks, "Then next time I suggest you get the fuck out my way."

"Look bitch, I was nice the first time, but don't think you're just gonna keep disrespecting me."

"Ohhhh, you gansta' all of a sudden, huh puta? Keep it up, 'cause I just loooove when little girls try to get tough. I guess you ain't hear what happened to the last broad who tried to test me."

"Leave her alone, Bella," Trinity meekly pleads.

"Awww that's cute," Bella laughs. "Your little sidekick is stickin' up for you."

"Ladies!" Lana sings, hurriedly entering the room, completely oblivious to the confrontation taking place, "I need you all on the floor now. Money, money, money!"

She continues into her office, leaving her door open.

"I know you think you're hot shit," Bella whispers to Fancy, "but there's only one Boriqua boss bitch up in here, and it sure as all fuck ain't you. Try me if you want, sweetheart. I will end your fucking career, and I ain't talkin' bout dancing."

Bella yanks Trinity's arm and she follows her into the bathroom, hanging her head low.

Chapter 29

It is the following day and since Fancy is off from work she's just lounging around the house. She is in the living room watching a woman give birth on "A Baby Story" when there is a knock at the door. She opens it and there on the doorstep she finds a bruised and battered Trinity, crying under her hooded sweatshirt.

"Oh my God, Trinity," she says, ushering her into the house. "What happened to you?"

"Me and Vin got into a fight."

"A fight? A grown man beating on a 110-pound girl is *not* a fight…it's abuse! Did you file a report with the police?"

"Hell no, Fancy! I ain't no damn snitch. It doesn't matter, anyway. We broke up. Only thing is I was living with him so I ain't got no place to stay now. So I was wondering if maybe I could stay with you for a couple weeks until I get myself together."

"Well you know this is my mom's house. I'll have to ask her."

"I don't have much money saved up, but here…"

Trinity hands Fancy three fifty-dollar bills.

"Wait right here while I talk to her."

Fancy goes upstairs and taps on Anna's door.

"Come in, Fancy," she says.

Fancy walks in and finds her mom ironing Rafael's clothes, while he lies in bed watching ESPN.

"Hey, Mom. Can I talk to you about something real quick?"

"Yeah, what is it?"

"It's kind of private. Can you step into the hall?"

"I'm in the middle of something, as you can see. So if you can't say it in front of Rafael, then it'll just have to wait."

Fancy doesn't see why it is so imperative for Anna to iron Rafael's clothes right this minute or, for that matter, why he is unable to iron his own, but since she's come to ask for a favor, she's not about to start an argument. She lets out a long huff before beginning.

"Well there's this young girl that I work with named Trinity. Me and her have become friends and she needs help."

"I hope you're not about to ask me for money, Fancy, because it's not happening. I'm broke."

"No, it's not that. She just needs a place to stay for a little while. She was living with her boyfriend but he started beating on her, so she left."

"I don't think so. Why can't she go to her parents?"

"She doesn't speak to them anymore. Come on, Mom. It'll only be for a few weeks so she can get back on her feet."

"Well Fancy, I'm sorry for your friend, but this is not a homeless shelter. I'm already supporting you. I can't handle any more financial responsibilities."

Fancy holds out the $150. Anna looks down at it, then at Fancy, then back at the money. She quickly snatches the money from Fancy's hand.

"Fine," Anna says. "She can stay in the back room. But only for a few weeks...no longer than that."

"Thanks, Mom. She's here now, so come out and meet her when you're done."

Fancy goes back downstairs and lets Trinity know it's okay for her to stay.

"Thanks, girl. I really appreciate it," she says, hugging Fancy.

"You're welcome. I wanted to ask you, though, what was going on between you and Bella yesterday? Why'd she grab you and pull you into the bathroom like that?"

"Oh that? That wasn't about nothing. She just asked me to switch shifts with her."

"So why was she all aggressive with you?"

"That's just how is she is. The bitch is mean. But on some real shit, you better watch out for her. I can see she's got it in for you, and I found out something bad about her."

"I don't care. I'm not gonna let her bully me. I'm a grown ass woman."

"Fancy, she's a Latin Queen."

"A Latin Queen?"

"Yeah, as in the gang. They're notorious for—"

"I know who they are, Trinity. And I know what they do. But why she got it in for me? I didn't do anything to that girl."

"Can't you see? She's jealous of you. She looks at you with pure hatred in her eyes. Please, Fancy, don't get into nothin' with her. She's dangerous."

"Well what the hell am I supposed to do? Quit Star's? That ain't gonna happen. I need this money."

"I don't know, but whatever you do, please take my advice: stay out of Bella's way."

Chapter 30

Fancy and Trinity walk into a run-down South Philadelphia row home and Fancy can't help but feel intimidated when she sees the party is packed with rowdy and drunken young men. They begin clapping and hollering loudly when the girls walk in.

"You said there would only be a *few* people here," Fancy says to Trinity who simply shrugs in response.

"Aye Rick, the hos here!" a sweaty shirtless man yells to another man who is in the kitchen. "Put some ass-shakin' music on!" Rick comes out of the kitchen holding a bottle of tequila and greets Trinity with a hug before setting up the music. An up-tempo song with heavy bass blares from two huge speakers on the floor and the whole house seems to shake.

"What the fuck y'all waitin' for?" the shirtless man asks, "We wanna see some ass!"

The other men clap and holler in agreement.

"Patience, fellas, patience!" Trinity says to the unruly men. "We just got here. We have to go change and get sexy for y'all."

Rick leads the ladies upstairs and shows them where they can change. They each swap their jeans and tops for skimpy two-pieces before heading back downstairs.

Vanna B.

Trinity starts dancing and collecting dollars. Although the men's rowdiness makes Fancy very uncomfortable, she follows suit and also begins to dance. The men start barking out demands.

"Take that thong off, ho!"

"Let's see some lesbo action!"

"Bust it open, bitch!"

In addition to their obscene demands, Fancy can feel their hands tugging at her clothes and touching her all over her body, making her more and more uncomfortable. Fancy decides enough is enough after the shirtless man puts his hand inside her panties.

"This is nuts," she says to Trinity. "I gotta get out of here."

The men boo in unison as Fancy dashes up the staircase.

"Just a sec, guys," Trinity yells, running up the stairs after her. "We'll be right back!"

"What are you doing?" Trinity asks Fancy. "We just got here."

"These dudes are too damn aggressive!"

"Stop acting like that, Fancy. Just have fun."

"This ain't fun to me. They're too wild. I'm not gonna stay here and be groped and called names. I'm out."

"You drawin'. If you wanna roll out then you're on your own. I'm staying here and gettin' this money."

While putting on her jeans, Fancy accidentally knocks over Trinity's bag. She is picking its contents up from the floor when she finds a Ziploc bag containing a mixture of pink and blue pills and several smaller bags of a white powder.

"Ohhh, now I see," Fancy says, holding up the drugs. "So this is why you suddenly know so much about Bella and her gang activities."

"Oh God," says Trinity, rolling her eyes. "I guess now you're gonna assume I'm a druggie and a horrible person. I just started snorting coke. And the E pills...well, I only take 'em when I'm working. I'm not addicted or anything."

"You're not addicted *yet*. Keep taking that shit and you will be."

"No I won't, Fancy. I know what I'm doing. I've just been stressed out lately. That's all. They help pick me up."

"Well look, I wanted to help you, but you're gonna have to find someplace else to stay. You can't be up in my mom's with that stuff. I'm sorry."

"I understand. It's cool – I was gonna ask Rick if I could move in here with him anyway. I'm sure he won't have a problem with it. He's been my homie for a long time. I appreciate your help, though. Thanks, big sis."

She reaches her arms out and gives Fancy a big hug.

"You're welcome. I just don't wanna see anything happen to you. I'll call you in the morning and you can come get your stuff."

Vanna B.

Fancy finishes dressing and walks out of the house with the men booing all the while. She walks down the dark, narrow street in the direction of Broad Street where she hopes to find a taxi. But before she can turn the corner off of the small street, someone grabs her arm. She spins around to see the shirtless man from the party. He's still not wearing a shirt and seems oblivious to the frigid night wind.

"Damn mami, why you leave?" he asks, reeking of liquor. "I didn't even get a chance to holla at you."

"Get off of my arm!" she says, trying to pull away from him. His grip is too strong, however, and she's unable to break free.

"Chillll, I know you datin'," says the man, pulling her closer. "How much?"

"Let go of me!" she screams, kicking him in his knee.

The man lets go of her arm and grabs his knee in pain.

"You fuckin' bitch!"

Fancy takes off running. She turns around to see the angry shirtless man closely in pursuit. He manages to grab onto her jacket and she falls to the ground, landing hard on her knee. The man grabs her by her hair, repeatedly punching her in the face as she struggles to get free. He kneels over her and begins trying to pull her pants down. Fancy refuses to submit and her attacker is unable to restrain her legs as she kicks furiously. Finally a kick catches him square in the face. Bleeding, he falls to the cold pavement in anguish, groaning and holding his gushing nose. Fancy runs as fast as she can and doesn't stop until she reaches brightly lit Broad Street.

After several minutes she is able to flag down a taxi.

"You alright?" the cab driver asks, looking at Fancy through the rear-view mirror.

"I'm fine. Please, just drive."

Once she is home Fancy goes into the bathroom to finally have a look at herself. She stares in the mirror at her bloody and swollen face, noticing her black eye and busted lip. She looks down at the scraped and bruised knee exposed through her torn jeans. Her head is pounding and she is missing a small chunk of hair from the side of her head. But Fancy doesn't care about any of that.

She lifts her shirt and gently rubs her belly, realizing she is actually very lucky; her attacker did not strike her stomach. Fancy is beyond grateful and knows that it is only through the grace of God that her unborn child remains unharmed. Despite the ordeal she has just endured, she considers herself blessed. *Thank God*.

She watches her reflection in the mirror as her eyes well up with tears. Not tears of joy, though; not even tears of sorrow; they are tears of *anger*.

"How could I endanger my baby like that?!" she sobs to herself. Fancy breathes deeply, attempting to fight back the rage rising up inside of her, but it is uncontainable. She makes a fist and strikes her reflection, shattering the mirror into pieces.

She storms to the hall closet for a trash bag, then into her room where she violently rummages through her closet and dresser drawers. She begins filling the trash bag with G-strings, bikinis, fishnet stockings and lace bodysuits – all of her stripping attire.

"I'm not an object or a ho or a slut!" she screams loudly. "And I'm not gonna let no disgusting perverts look at or touch or grab my body ever again!"

Fancy doesn't stop after the dancewear. She continues throwing items in the bag: Seven jeans, Fendi bags, Louboutin shoes, even her favorite Herve Leger dress.

"Fuck this shit! I don't need it. I'm not gonna be a slave to these bullshit labels anymore!"

Fancy stops when she finds the Gucci items she bought for the baby. Knowing they are for her little angel, she cannot bring herself to throw them away. She just holds them close and smiles. Thinking of the baby calms her down. But by then it is too late. Fancy's ranting has already awakened her mother, who briskly stomps over and flings open the door.

"Fancy, what the hell is wrong with you?" Anna asks angrily. "It's 2 AM!"

"Sorry, Mom. I just realized I'm tired of all this."

"Of what?!"

"Everything! The strip club, the designer crap – this is not me! I just wanna be me! I guess you can say in cleaning out my closet, I'm also cleansing my soul."

Fancy shrugs and smiles an awkward smile. Anna looks at her, puzzled. Then she notices Fancy's battered face.

"Oh my God, what happened to you? Are you okay?"

"Yeah, I'm okay. Actually, I'm better than okay. I'm alive!"

Anna looks at Fancy in bewilderment.

"Who did this to you?" she asks.

"It doesn't matter, Mom. It was a wake-up call – a much-needed one. I have to get my life together for this baby. I can't work at that club anymore. And I hope you don't mind if I stay here just a little longer because—"

"Of course you can stay," Anna interrupts. "You think I would put my own daughter out on the street? Well, maybe I would, but not with my grandchild."

Anna and Fancy laugh together.

"You can stay as long as you want, but you have to be respectful of me and my life. Okay?"

"Okay."

"What do you plan on doing with all that stuff?" Anna asks, pointing to the overflowing trash bag.

"Take it. I don't need it. Give it to someone who can use it."

"Ok, Fancy."

"No. No more Fancy, Mom. I'm Maribel."

Anna smiles.

"Okay, Mari."

Anna and Maribel hug and for a moment both mother and daughter feel a genuine warmth they have not felt between them in a very long time.

After such a night Maribel is glad to be safely in her bed. She lies curled up, the softness of her sheets caressing her skin. She snuggles her throbbing head against her pillow, which, for the first time ever, she realizes she appreciates, for even though it is lumpy, it is a soft place to lay her head. Her bed feels more comfortable than ever.

"Thank you, Jesus" she whispers, smiling in the dark, and after a long pause adds, "Please let my Mom be understanding about the mirror."

Chapter 31

When Maribel wakes up in the morning she dials Trinity's number.

"Hey," she answers sleepily.

"Trinity, oh my God, last night was crazy. When I left the house this guy attacked me and tried to rape me."

"What? Are you serious? What guy?"

"That guy from the party that had his shirt off."

"Oh my God. That was one of Rick's friend's cousins. They were looking for him. He disappeared and nobody knew what happened to him. Are you okay?"

"Yeah, I'm alright. He beat me up pretty bad but the baby's okay, thank God."

"I feel so bad, man. I shouldn't have put you in that situation. I should have taken you home. I just—"

"Don't worry about it. It's over now. Did you talk to Rick about you staying there?"

"Yeah, he said it's cool. Can I come get my stuff in like an hour?"

"Yeah, that's fine. Can you give me a ride down to Star's afterwards?"

"You workin' the day shift?"

"Nah, I'm quitting. I can't be doing that dancing shit any more. That life ain't for me, especially being pregnant and all."

"I feel you. Yeah I'll take you over there."

After breaking the news to Lana about her decision to leave Star's, Fancy goes to collect her things from her locker. As she is doing so, Bella walks in the dressing room to prepare for her shift.

"Damn," she laughs, noticing Maribel's battered face. "So that's why you and Trinity are such good friends. You both like to get your asses whooped."

"Look, says Maribel, "I don't know what your problem is with me and I honestly don't care. But for you to be corrupting a girl as young as Trinity, that's just fucked up, Bella. I'm asking you woman to woman, please stop dealing to her. She has a lot going on and she needs her head on straight."

"So you think you can just walk up in here telling me what to do and it's gonna happen just like that," she says, snapping her fingers. "I do what the fuck I want when I want."

"Well what if I was to tell Lev that you're selling to his girls? Or better yet, what if I went to the police?"

In a flash, Bella pulls a knife from her bag and has Maribel pinned against her locker with the six-inch, double-edge blade at her throat.

"I guess you don't know what happens to snitches."

"Bella, please." Fancy says, petrified and trembling with fear. "I didn't mean it. I'm not gonna tell – I was just talking shit. I'm leaving Star's now. Let me go and you'll never see me again."

Bella laughs and then finally backs away from Maribel, putting the knife back in her bag.

"Oh I wouldn't bank on that. You can run away all you want, but trust me princesa, you haven't seen the last of Bella."

Maribel quickly collects her belongings and hurries back to the car where Trinity is waiting to take her back home.

"I ran into Bella."

"What happened?" asks Trinity, noticing Maribel appears somewhat shaken up.

"She put a fuckin' knife to my throat and threatened me."

"What?!"

"I told her to stop selling you drugs."

"Why the hell would you do that? I told you to stay out her way and all you do is keep picking fights with her. You're gonna get hurt messing with that girl. You wanna have all the Latin Kings and Queens in the city on your ass? When you beef with one of them you beef with them all. You do NOT want that, especially with a baby on the way."

"I know. We'll I quit now, so hopefully I won't see her anymore."

Maribel thanks Trinity for the ride before heading in the house and up to her room. She takes a business card off her dresser and dials the number on it. She presses the phone against her ear and paces while the other end of the line rings. After the fourth ring she is preparing to hang up when finally, someone answers.

"Hello?"

"Hi, Lou. I don't know if you remember me, but we met at Star's. My name is—"

"Fancy. Yeah, I remember you."

"Oh, good...I'm glad you do. But actually, you can call me Maribel – that's my real name."

"Maribel, huh? Yes, I like that much better than Fancy."

"Well, I was calling to see if your offer was still available."

"The job offer? Yes, of course. I'm a man of my word. What part of the city are you in, Maribel?"

"I live in Olney. I'm actually only a few blocks from your store on 6th Street."

"Okay, that's good. So how soon can you start?"

"I can start as soon as tomorrow if you already have a position available."

"Sure. I'll have Angie start training you as a cashier tomorrow, then. How's 11 AM sound?"

"That's perfect."

"Alright, I'll see you then."

"Thanks, Lou. See you tomorrow."

Chapter 32

Maribel has been working at Val-U Rite for a few days now, and she's discovered the job actually is not as bad as she expected. In fact, she appreciates the simplicity and predictability of it. She enjoys conversing with the customers and performs her job with a smile.

She is on her lunch break one day, when she decides to give Trinity a call.

"Hey, girl," Trinity answers cheerfully. "How you doin'?"

"Hey! I'm good. How are you?"

"I'm straight. Same ol' same ol'. Working at Star's, tryna make a couple dollars. What you been up to?"

"I've been working, too. I got a cashier job at Val-U Rite."

"Val-U Rite?"

"Yeah, remember that little supermarket around the corner from my mom's that we went to that time?"

"Oh yeah. How do you like it?"

"It's actually not too bad. The pay is lower, of course, but at least I don't have to worry about any drama, like at Star's."

"You ain't neva lie."

Maribel's main reason for calling is to see if Bella has said anything to Trinity about her since she left. But since Trinity has not mentioned it during their conversation, she figures she must not have. She supposes Bella has forgotten all about her and that her threats must have been just that – merely verbal bluffs delivered with no actual intent to act. Maribel is relieved – a load has been lifted from her mind.

"Well alright, Trin. I just wanted to see how you were doing. We should link up this weekend. We can grab a bite to eat or something."

"Cool, sounds good. I'll call you Saturday."

"K. Talk to you later."

"Bye."

Chapter 33

The next day Maribel works the late shift. When she is finished ringing up her final customer, she counts her drawer and prepares to leave. As she is exiting the store, she looks at her phone and sees eight missed calls, five voicemails and four text messages, all from Trinity. *Something must be wrong*, Maribel thinks. *I hope Trinity is okay.* She quickly reads the first text message:

Bella is coming to your job! Don't walk home alone! I'm so sorry.

But by then it is too late. Maribel looks up from her phone and is face to face with Bella. Her heart feels like it has leapt up in her throat and she begins to sweat. In her right hand Bella is holding the same knife she held to Maribel's throat just days ago.

"Hey pretty girl," Bella says with a demonic grin. "Let's see how fancy you look with your face sliced up."

Maribel slowly backs up and is startled when she unexpectedly bumps into someone. She turns her head slightly, glancing over her shoulder, and out of the corner of her eye she sees a girl with bright red hair. The girl pushes Maribel hard and she stumbles to her right and into another girl who glares at her angrily. When Maribel looks to her left she sees yet another of Bella's gang members.

Maribel is surrounded with nowhere to run. The redhead pushes her again, this time so hard she falls back and hits her head on the ground. She kicks Maribel in her back, causing her to scream out in pain. Maribel curls into a ball, attempting to protect her stomach. As Bella and her three girl-goons move in on her, Maribel pleads for their mercy.

"Leave me alone! Stop! Please don't hurt me! Pleeeease!"

Bella stands over Maribel peering down at her for a moment before yanking her up by her hair. She raises the knife up to Maribel's cheek. Maribel closes her eyes tightly, bracing herself for the pain that Bella is about to inflict on her.

BANG!

A single gunshot is fired and Bella and her crew scatter. A police car parked only two blocks away, begins in the direction of the gunshot. The loudening siren and swirling blue and red lights are quickly approaching. Maribel turns to see Trinity standing by the grocery store frantically tucking a gun in the waistband of her pants.

"Fancy!" she yells out to her. "Come over here, quick!" They run behind the store and disappear down the dark back street where Trinity is parked. When the police arrive they find the Latin Queens running through the parking lot.

Trinity and Maribel get in the car and start toward her mother's house. Maribel's heart is still pounding and Trinity's hands tremble as she tries to hold the wheel steady.

"You sold me out!" Maribel yells angrily, out of breath. "I can't believe you told her where I work!"

"I'm sorry, Fancy! She threatened me. What was I supposed to do? I didn't wanna tell her where you lived, but I had to give her something. She had a knife to my throat!"

"After all this time you telling me how dangerous Bella is and to watch out for her and then you go behind my back, putting me and my baby in danger!"

"Fancy, I tried to warn you. And I came to help you, didn't I? That's gotta count for something."

"What if you didn't make it in time, huh? They might have killed me."

"Well they didn't."

"This ain't the end of it, you know. She's gonna keep coming after me. She's crazy!"

Chapter 34

It turns out that there was a warrant out for Bella's arrest. When the police caught her, they arrested her and, lucky for Maribel, she's been in jail ever since.

It's been almost four months since the incident and Maribel has all but forgotten about Bella and her close call with the Latin Queens. Things have been the best they've been in a long time for her. When she started working at the market, she began helping her mother out with bills and expenses, and thus their relationship has somewhat improved. Anna broke up with Rafael and since he moved out, she and Maribel have been converting the back room into a nursery for the baby. In eradicating all the drama in her life, Maribel was forced to cut all ties with Trinity. She is still enjoying her job at Val-U Rite and is usually friendly and smiling while working. Today, however, instead of her usual bright smile, she is sporting a frown that, every so often, morphs into a painful grimace. One of her regular customers, a heavyset Dominican woman named Maria, immediately notices Maribel is not herself.

"Que pasa, Maribel?" Maria asks with a concerned look. "You feeling okay? You don't look so good."

"I'm fine, Maria," Fancy says, rubbing her large, round baby bump. "Just been having some really bad cramps lately."

"Those aren't cramps, mami. You're having contractions. Looks like the baby is coming soon."

"Nah, I'm not due for another two-and-a-half weeks," Fancy says, bagging the last of Maria's groceries.

"I don't think the little one's gonna wait that long. Hasta luego."

"Bye."

There isn't anyone in line behind Maria so Maribel is able to take a break. She unfolds the metal chair that Lou thoughtfully provided for her, and gives her swollen, achy feet a break. She doubles over as the pain in her abdomen intensifies.

"You aight?" a familiar voice says from the other side of the conveyor belt.

Fancy looks up to put a face with the voice, and staring down at her is one of her old party companions.

"Brittany?"

"Fancy?"

"No," Maribel says defensively. "It's Maribel."

"You work here?"

"Yeah. What are you doing around here?"

"I'm headed downtown. You know I take the Boulevard to 76."

"Oh, yeah."

"I had a little emergency so I had to make a pit stop," Brittany says, pointing to the box of tampons on the conveyor belt.

Maribel scans the box and Brittany hands her the money.

"Where's the bathroom, Fan— I mean Mari—...Marisol was it?"

"It's Maribel...and the bathroom's over there."

"Okay, Maribel. This is weird as shit. All that time I thought Fancy was your real name."

Brittany laughs and yells "be right back" as she jogs to the ladies' room. Maribel rolls her eyes.

"For what?" she mumbles under her breath. It is awkward seeing Brittany. After her last unpleasant run-in with Jaslyn and Aaron, and especially since her epiphany, she had hoped she wouldn't have to face anyone from her past again. They were bound to bombard her with questions she simply didn't wish to answer. She had turned over a new leaf and she did not want to revisit the past. She hopes that Brittany will just leave after exiting the bathroom, but instead of walking toward the door she walks back over to her register. Maribel huffs and slouches down in her metal folding chair, bracing herself for a conversation she is not in the mood to have.

"So yeah, girl, you just disappeared. I was wondering what happened to you."

Brittany waits for Maribel to respond, but instead is met with a cold, blank stare.

"I see you about ready to pop. Not much longer now, huh?"

"Nope."

"You not staying in the Piazza no more?"

"Nah."

Maribel figures Brittany gets the picture when she begins fishing around in her purse for her keys.

"Well aight, girl," Brittany says. "It was good seeing you. We'll have to get together ASAP...maybe hit up Posh or something. You still got my number, right?"

"Yeah," Maribel lies.

"Let me get yours. I don't think I have it anymore."

Maribel reluctantly gives Brittany her number, figuring she probably won't call, but still she finds herself immediately regretting it.

"Well call me if you need anything," Brittany says, turning and walking toward the door.

"Brittany!" Maribel yells after her.

Brittany spins around to see Maribel's eyes are as wide as those of a deer caught in headlights.

"I need a ride," she says, frozen in fear. "My water just broke!"

Chapter 35

Brittany's Porsche speeds toward Albert Einstein Hospital with Maribel panicking on the passenger side. Whenever she is experiencing contractions Maribel grips the Italian leather dashboard and screams in agony. Between contractions is her only chance to gather her thoughts and a thousand things are running through her head:

My God, I can't wait to get to the hospital and get some drugs! I knew it would be painful, but it's even worse than I expected. If it hurts this bad already, what's it gonna feel like when the baby is actually coming out?! I can't believe I'm really about to give birth! Please don't let it be in this tiny ass coupe. I never imagined I'd be riding to the hospital in Brittany's car. How random is this? Out of the blue she just shows up at the market and, boom! – my water breaks. Some timing she has. Aw, shit...here comes another damn contraction!

Maribel squeals like a stuck pig. She finally breaks down into tears.

"I'm not gonna make it!" she cries. "I can't handle this!"

When the pain subsides Maribel looks out the window and notices that Brittany is going the wrong way.

"What the fuck, Brit? Why you getting on the expressway? The hospital is on Old York Road."

"We're taking a detour," Brittany says flatly, looking straight ahead at the road.

"What? Come on, man. This ain't the time to be playin'. I'm having a fucking baby here! Get off at the next exit."

When Brittany drives past the exit Fancy really begins to get scared. She takes out her phone to call for help, but Brittany snatches it and throws it out the window. Maribel grabs the wheel.

"Stop the goddamn car! Pull over, now!"

"Let go of the wheel before you kill us both!"

"No! I'm not gonna let go. Pull the fuck over!"

The car swerves as they fight over the wheel. Passing drivers honk their horns and shout out obscenities as they serve out of the way to avoid being hit by the erratic Porsche. Finally the car skids to the shoulder and crashes into a guardrail. Maribel gets out and immediately starts running up the side of the highway, waving her hands wildly, hoping someone will stop to help her.

A maroon van pulls over and the middle-aged woman inside rolls down the passenger side window.

"Are you okay?"

"No, I'm in labor! I need to get to the hospital!"

"Okay, get in. I'll take you."

"Thank you so much," Maribel says, once inside.

"Were you in that Porsche that crashed back there? Are you injured?"

"Yeah, I was. But no, I'm fine other than these contractions.

"What happened?"

"You'll probably think I'm crazy if I tell you."

Chapter 36

Back on the shoulder of I-76E Brittany is pulling off in her crashed Porsche, making a phone call.

"How'd it go?" the deep male voice on the other end asks.

"Terrible...a disaster."

"She don't wanna deal with you?"

"Worse. Craziest thing happened. I went in and the bitch went into labor while I was standing there!"

"You gotta be kidding me. So what happened?"

"Well, I saw it as an opportunity. She asked me to take her to the hospital so I was just gonna bring her to you."

"Bring her to me?! For what?!"

"So you could off her! Wasn't that the whole point of me trying to get cool with her again?"

"You fuckin' idiot! I'm not gonna do it myself. I can't get my hands dirty. I got a damn career."

"Well how the hell was I supposed to know?"

"I can't believe how dumb you are. Why the hell would you...never mind. So you're on your way here with her?"

"Well I was but..."

"But what, Brittany?"

"We sort of had a little accident. She grabbed the wheel and we banged out."

"Oh my God. So where are you now?"

"I'm on 76, but she ran off down the highway. Somebody picked her up and I guess they're taking her to the hospital."

"I can't believe this shit! I sent you to do a simple ass task. All you had to do was make friends with her again, get her to trust you and I would've had her taken care of later—"

"There wasn't gonna be no later! I told you the bitch went into labor! That was the only way I could think of how to get it done before the damn baby was born."

"What the fuck am I supposed to do now?"

"I don't know, man. We'll think of something. I'm on way over there now. See you soon, Aaron."

To be continued...

About the Author

Vanna B. is from Philadelphia and holds a Bachelor of Arts in journalism from Temple University. Prior to writing *Fancy*, she worked as a staff and freelance writer/columnist for numerous publications. Her hobbies include music, movies, reading, fitness and ballroom dancing.

www.VannaBOnline.com
www.Twitter.com/MsVannaB
www.Facebook.com/VannaBOnline